THE TRACK OF THE ASSASSIN

Something metallic, a silver tube with a lens at one end, glittered near the stunned girl. Óin took it up, and his oversized grip depressed the stud.

The finger-thick scarlet thread gouged a foot-long scar in the ground before Óin realized it was a weapon and turned it on the Guildsman. The laser swept the side of the alley, cutting a wavering gash the length of the wall. It scored the ribs of the Guildsman as he twisted desperately aside, trying to evade it.

Óin didn't wait to see if he made it. He grabbed the girl up under one arm and ran for the end of the alleyway, away from the flames and the Guildsman. There was a shabby fence blocking access to the street beyond. Óin went at it at a dead run, and jumped. . . .

D1329047

Also from Orbit by Richard S. McEnroe:

THE SHATTERED STARS

RICHARD S. McENROE

Flight of Honour

Futura

An Orbit Book

020695536

Copyright © 1984 by Richard McEnroe

Portions of this novel appeared in somewhat different form in Isaac Asimov's Science Fiction Magazine (May 1980) under the title 'Wolkenheim Fairday'.

First published in 1984 in the USA by Bantam Books

This edition published in 1986
by Futura Publications, a Division of
Macdonald & Co (Publishers) Ltd
London & Sydney

All rights reserved
No part of this publication may be reproduced, stored in a retrieval system, or transmitted, in any form or by any means without the prior permission in writing of the publisher, nor be otherwise circulated in any form of binding or cover other than that in which it is published and without a similar condition including this condition being imposed on the subsequent purchaser.

All characters in this publication are fictitious and any resemblance to real persons, living or dead, is purely coincidental.

ISBN 0 7088 8190 4

Printed and bound in Great Britain by
Cox & Wyman Ltd, Reading

Futura Publications
A Division of
Macdonald & Co (Publishers) Ltd
Greater London House
Hampstead Road
London NW1 7QX
A BPCC plc Company

DEDICATIONS

*To George, Shawna & The Good Doctor, for
seeing the story in Óin Ceiragh
and
To Nick Yermakov, for Ten Years of mutual support and nudzhery. Maybe it's still the best thing
I ever wrote, now that I've finished it.*

WEST LANCASHIRE
DISTRICT LIBRARIES

W/K 2/02	W/B
W/O	W/A
W/U	M/L
T/L	WR 5/87

Part One

LEAVE–TAKING

Chapter One

He stood atop the earthen parapet, a squat, powerful creature that might have been cut from the heartstone of the hills before him. But not even the unearthly gravity of his world had made his shoulders so broad that they could bear the burden of the grief that overwhelmed him. His three-fingered hands worked of their own accord, gouging deeply into the packed soil of the parapet.

Cian Canbhei raged at the new day dawning before him.

Bright *edhean* rose in golden splendor above the broad forests surrounding Canbhei Holding, driving back the night, heralding the first morning of a world that had no place in it for Cian Canbhei.

The sheer ordinariness of it appalled him. His life had collapsed around him, and yet *edhean* rose at his appointed time, the sky was as clear and blue as he had ever seen it, and the free-holders and hearth-bonds in the distant fields assailed the cane-stands with the minute industry of observed insects, a purposefulness inconceivable to Cian in his grief.

He turned his back on the orderly, deceitful landscape below him, to look back into the courtyard of the Holding. Here at least was a scene to match his own emotional desolation: the courtyard was deserted, whereas it should have been bustling with the morning's

3

activity. Troughs were unfilled, the tanning racks in the open sheds unattended, the hides left unscraped and slack, the kilns and ovens, jutting out from the rough stone walls of the hold itself, unfired and empty. The hearth-bonds and family that should have been tending them were absent, gathered for the funeral vigil within the hold.

And he should have been with them. Cian moved back from the earthen, grass-covered parapet, reluctantly descending the angled ramp to the flagstoned courtyard.

The sudden shaft of daylight striking through the shadowed great hall as Cian slipped through the door seemed almost as jarring as a bray of derisive laughter might have been. Several people turned, glaring angrily as the light fell across the face of dead Fen upon his bier, the sudden play of brightness and shadow there lending a brief, false animation to those still features. But the anger fled as they recognized Cian, replaced by pity for the bereaved son, a pity that twisted Cian's soul almost as much as did his own grief. He was *gal-adheni*, and there was no pride in being pitied.

The crowd parted as Cian advanced on the bier. At least no one offered him any consolations, he thought bitterly; at least they spared him that.

Cianna and Dhein stood aside as he came to the bier. The iron gorget of Cianna's new station looked strange, loose around her neck: there had been no time yet to have it properly fitted. The fastenings were still sized for the neck of their dead father before them, though in full accordance with proper tradition, his golden badge had been stripped from him and passed to his heir before the body was even cold. Cianna seemed uncomfortable with its weight around her neck, almost as uncomfortable as Cian felt seeing it there. Dhein had retreated within the formal privacy of her hooded acolyte's robes, but her seeming composure offered no affront. She was *sgeadhan*, or nearly, and her calling gave her the strength of accession to the state of things,

4

her recognition of their unfathomable workings. Cian envied her the solace of her wisdom, even as he failed utterly to grasp it.

He reached the bier and looked down on the body of his dead father. The broken limbs had been straightened, as best they might. The release of death had erased the deep line of pain from that weathered, knowing face; the three-fingered hands lay relaxed and still at Fen Canbhei's sides, in sharp contrast to the hands with which Cian gripped the edges of the bier, white-knuckled, tendons working like serpents beneath their skin. He wrenched futilely at the blackstone surface of the bier as though he would forcibly drag the life back into his father. But it was too late for that, and too great a task for his feeble strength. If the vitality, the once-unquenchable *sgeadhanha-dan* of Fen Canbhei had been unequal to the onslaught of tons of plummeting stone, there was nothing his son could do to put the imbalance aright.

He felt a presence by his side: Cianna and Dhein, who had moved up quietly beside him. He retreated a step from the bier, hands raised in warding.

"No," he said. "Not now. Not yet."

"It has to be, Cian," his older sister said.

"Please," he begged, hating himself for his weakness, for making it harder than it already was.

"Cian," she said, his name a reminder and a hidden plea. Cian felt something within himself snap and fall away, leaving only emptiness.

"*Ai, shta,*" he cursed softly, too quietly for even those gathered at the front of the assembly to hear. He moved stiffly to the end of the bier, as Dhein joined him there.

Cianna reached down and drew the edge of the scarlet funerary shroud up over the face of their father. She smoothed the cloth and grasped the end of the blackstone slab. When she looked up and met their gaze, Cian and Dhein reached down, in turn, and gripped the end before them.

The three raised the corpse of their father, and the waiting attendants drew back the larger scarlet hanging that covered the mouth of the great hall hearth. It had been scrubbed down to bare stone, gleaming as if no fire had ever been lit within it. Kindling and seasoned logs had been arranged within it and soaked thoroughly with thick, scented oil.

The bier was heavy in Cian's hands, even with his sister to help him. But Cianna lifted her end without expression, refusing to let the effort register in her face, even as she suppressed her grief. They carried their father to the waiting hearth and set the blackstone bier upon the iron supports prepared for it.

Cian and Dhein stepped back the proper ten paces from the hearth and crossed before it, then moved forward again to stand beside their sister. More attendants stepped forward, handing them the brands already burning. The fire in his hands seemed to mesmerize Cian Canbhei.

Half a dozen figures stepped forward out of the crowd: quarrymen, in whose workings Fen Canbhei had died. They bore their finest tools with them, polished until they shone as they had not shone since the day of their first forging. One by one they placed the tools, picks, and long-hafted hammers and heavy wedges among the logs beneath Fen Canbhei. One elder among them laid his pick down with the rest and then fell to his knees, seamed hands gripping the edge of the bier, forehead pressed to it, patently offering a more personal sacrifice.

"No, Belin," Cianna said gently, the quiet sound of her voice shocking Cian from his reverie. The old quarryman looked up at her with fierce, ravaged eyes.

"Please, *aya*," he said broken-voiced. "On my head this is; in my works—"

"Belin," Cianna said. "Your lord himself would have rebuked you for such wastefulness. The *sgeadhanha-dan* of stone is its own, and my father's, his. If this is how

6

they were to meet, then no one is to blame. This is not needful."

Belin stared up at her a moment longer, then rose and fled back into the crowd.

Cianna Canbhei stepped forward, her sister Dhein behind her, and Cian last. She laid her brand down among the piled kindling, as did Dhein, and Cian, gripping his brand two-handed and flinging it down as though striking at an enemy he could never hope to overcome.

The flames blossomed swiftly, the oil-soaked wood catching at once, and within seconds the body of Fen Canbhei was lost to sight within the fire as his ashes merged with the stone of the hold he had made strong. The fire would be allowed to burn itself out in its own time, and all within the holding would fast until that time. Then the bier would be removed and a new hearth-fire kindled, and life for the Canbhei would begin anew under Cianna their lord, *adhe* keep her.

The children of Fen Canbhei stood vigil over the pyre. Cianna gripped the gorget around her neck as though drawing strength from the iron itself. Dhein stood upright with folded hands, her composure belied by the tracks of the tears that coursed down her cheeks.

And Cian Canbhei screamed a scream of inarticulate denial and fled the great hall, into the pitiless glare of the new day.

"I would leave," Cian said.

The words sounded unreal, even to him. There were things a *gal-adheni* simply did not say, much less do—there were things a *gal-adheni* could not even say *properly*, for his actual, physical departure from Canbhei Holding was the least part of what Cian hoped to convey.

"Where are you going?" Cianna asked, not paying him her whole attention, for the southwestern fields were showing an unexpectedly diminished harvest that year, and she needed to decide whether to order them rotated a season earlier than planned, with all the confusion that would cause in the schedules for the rest of the fields.

"I mean to take service with the Consortium Mercantile," Cian said.

"What?" Cianna looked up sharply from her accounts, grain yields and soil fixes forgotten.

"I mean to take service with Consortium," Cian said, "aboard one of the great ships when next they call."

"Brother, are you mad?" Cianna came out from behind her table to face him more closely. The light from the tall, narrow window caught her from the side, and this close to her, Cian could now see the new lines care and work had etched at the corners of her eyes. The fastenings to her gorget of office had been taken up; now it bound her throat tightly. "Would you divorce yourself from the very flesh of *adhe* herself?"

"Would I? No," Cian said. "But must I? I feel I have to."

"Is it the death of our father, then, that has brought you to this?"

"In large part," Cian admitted, "*adhe* grant him peace. But that is not the whole of it."

"Then what is?"

"I must leave," Cian said, choosing his words carefully, "because of what the death of Fen has left of Cian Canbhei."

"And what is that?"

"Nothing that I can see," said Cian Canbhei.

"Creac's heart, brother. You talk madness—"

"No," said Cian. "No, Cianna, I'm speaking of something I only see clearly now, for the first time." He moved to the window and the short, low bench there and sat, not looking at her. "What am I?"

"You are Cian Canbhei—"

"*What* am I? Not *who* am I. I know my name, sister. It is all I am sure of."

Cianna watched him carefully as she spoke. "You

8

are my brother, Cian, and Dhein's, whom we love. You are the son of Fen Canbhei—"

"Just so," said Cian. "I am your brother and Dhein's, and I was my father's son. But I am nothing of my own."

"I don't understand."

"I am just as you have described me. I am something of yours, of Dhein's, of my father's. But how would you describe me other than by naming me a possession of another?"

"You are the second-born of our line. Had I not lived, you would be hold-lord now—"

"But you are hold-lord now, Cianna, and the succession will pass through your children. So to be second-born has no meaning, no value. No purpose. But that is what I mean. You are hold-lord now. That is what Cianna Canbhei is, and what she contributes to our clan. And Dhein is *sgeadhan*, or will be. That is what Dhein Canbhei is, and what she contributes to our clan. But Cian Canbhei is nothing. *I* am nothing, and I contribute nothing. I never contributed anything, save my presence against the possibility that the clan might be deprived of a more direct succession. That contribution is not needed anymore—and I have nothing to offer in its place."

"That is not true. You have learning, you have skill at arms, you have courage—"

"And I have pride. Or arrogance, perhaps. There are wiser Canbhei, more fell Canbhei, and I should think none of our name lack for courage. Shall I subordinate myself to them? I do not believe the blood of Fen Canbhei would permit that. Even to you, sister, for though you are loved in your turn, we have been peers too long for me to humble myself before you now."

"I could never want that."

"But it is all I have to offer you, do you see? That is all this Cian Canbhei can give—servitude. And that is no fit offering for a Canbhei. So I must find a new Cian

9

Canbhei or remake this old one, and to do that, I must seek out the Consortium."

"But *gal-adheni* who enter the service of the Consortium do not return."

"Some do."

"So many do not, Cian."

"But one who did would at least be fit to bear our name, Cianna. What else can I do? Where else could I go? Should I make of myself a hearth-bond to the Jeadhanim or the Kenselagh? Do they deserve a Canbhei for a servant?"

"No. But a Canbhei does not deserve to die because of the weight of his name."

"I do not mean to die. But if I am to live as a Canbhei, I must be more than something of another's."

"I could forbid this, Cian."

"And I would honor your will. But that would change nothing. And this will not pass, not for me, unless I act upon it. I ask that you understand this."

"*Adhe* forgive me, Cian, yes, I do. Have you decided when you will go?"

"I see no reason to wait. As soon as I can make ready."

"Then you had best start. . . ."

"Yes." Cian shook his head. "Perhaps this would be easier for me if you resisted it more."

Cianna shook her head sadly. "If there is one thing I hope I inherited along with this heavy damned collar, let it be the wisdom to know when not to give a command that cannot be obeyed. Your *sgeadhanha-dan* is plain to me, Cian. You must have it thus."

"That wisdom is yours. Yet your anger might at least give me something to oppose, some point from which to orient myself in this void that claims me."

"Then I will fail you. I cannot find it within me to rage at you for something neither of us may change."

Dhein found him in his room. He had gotten as far as laying out his cloak and his best boots, but his ruck lay flaccid and empty upon his bed, surrounded by a scatter of curios and possessions.

"Second thoughts?" Dhein asked.

"Too many first ones," Cian answered glumly. "I'm trying to compress an entire life into something I can carry on my back, and it isn't working." He picked up the small wooden flute, remembering the care with which old Stane had worked on the small keys and stops to give it a greater range than six fingers could play unaided, regretting that his small gift for music had never equaled the craft that had gone into its making. He laid the flute aside and lifted up the carefully bound, illuminated book of clan tales. He should take that, he thought, or something like it, to remind him of what he was. But he knew every story the book could tell him, had committed them to memory before he'd ever grown his first beard, and it seemed almost sacrilegious to submit something so precious to the rigors of travel, as well as whatever perils he faced, unknowing, out in the Consortium. Besides, he had to find out now what those stories meant for him, and there was no book that could help him with that. He set the book down beside the flute.

"I assume Cianna sent you to whip my *sgeadhanhadan* back into proper shape, didn't she?" he asked.

"I wouldn't presume to try," Dhein answered him. "I barely understand my own as yet. Besides, that's a task for yourself alone, Cian."

"It's good that someone sees that, at least."

He laid the long Canbhei cane-knife atop his cloak without hesitation. The heavy-bladed, square-edged knife was the true Canbhei tool, which reaped the sweet, strong cane that was their livelihood and defended the land they had made their own. No Canbhei would ever go abroad without it.

"As long as that is what you're doing," Dhein said.

"I'm not interested in scholar's games of logic," Cian said, more sharply than he'd meant to.

"Neither am I, right now. But you'd better get used

11

to them, Cian. You'll be playing them every day that you're gone."

"No, I won't," he said. "What I'll be doing is serving the Consortium as best I can until I've gained enough wealth and a good enough reputation to come back and start a holding of my own, as a true Canbhei."

"Is that why you're doing this? For wealth and fame, then?"

"No. But those are what I need, just now, if I am to make of myself something worth being."

"But you must fear the mysteries of the Consortium—"

"Of course, sister. But I have to face them."

"Then why won't you stay here?"

"What?"

"You are willing to face the Consortium, not knowing what it may hold in store for you out there. But you flee your own home. What do you fear here?"

"This is my home. There is nothing to fear here."

"Then why leave?"

"Creac's eyes, Dhein! I thought you wouldn't presume to influence my *sgeadhanha-dan!* Your own words."

"I will not. I don't presume to possess such wisdom. But I would do what I can to help you understand it. Because that is where your real danger lies."

"What are you talking about?"

"What do you fear here?"

"Nothing!"

"Then why leave?"

"We could talk in such circles all day if I let us. I'm leaving because there's nothing for me here, Dhein. There is nothing Cian Canbhei can give to the clan. There is no *reason* for Cian Canbhei to be here."

"We would not have you leave."

"That is something you give me. And I have nothing I can return for it."

"We don't ask for anything, Cian."

"I ask for something of myself. I have to."

"And so you will go out into the Consortium to find this something?"

"I don't know where else to look, Dhein."

"What will you give the Consortium, then, that you cannot give us?"

"I don't know yet."

"And what can they give you that we cannot?"

"I don't know that, either. Dammit, Dhein, do you think these are questions I have not asked myself? Why must you worry at them, as well?"

"You do not know what the Consortium can give you to give us that you cannot give us yourself. And you do not know what you can give them that you cannot give us."

Cian smiled wryly. "You make my *sgeadhanha-dan* out to be a murky one."

Dhein shook her head soberly. "Even with what little I have learned, that is not so. *Sgeadhanha* is never unclear; what truly is can never be in doubt. It is only our perceptions of it that may be confused."

"Then what is my *sgeadhanha-dan*, wise little sister?"

"You do not know what you can offer the Consortium."

"All right."

"And you do not know what you can offer us."

"If anything. But continue, please."

"You do not even know if they are the same thing, do you?"

"How can I? No, I do not."

"Then why not search for them here, among those who love you and would help you look? Think, Cian. Why go so far abroad to look for something that might be right here within you?"

He could not face her. Finally, he answered uncertainly: "Sister . . . what if I looked here—and failed?" She did not answer him. "How could I face you then, with my worthlessness writ large between us? What service could I offer to our line then?"

13

"And is that why you would leave us? That fear?"

"I am Canbhei," Cian said hotly. "I do not flee from things that frighten me, like a child."

"And yet you will leave us."

"To *find* something, Dhein—not to leave something behind. Can't you see that?"

Dhein Canbhei looked at him sadly. "I see that there is something you have to look for," she agreed, "and I see that I lack the wit to make you see it for what it is . . . and yet it may not be part of your *sgeadhan-ha-dan* that you ever learn yourself. I hope I am yet unskilled enough to be wrong in that, as well. *Adhe* keep you, brother."

And with that she was gone, leaving Cian alone among the relics of his forsaken past.

They were waiting for him at the gate.

The hearth-bonds in the courtyard went about their business, ignoring him as he passed among them. It was a family matter, among direct blood-kin alone, and something in which they had no place.

Everything seemed unnaturally vivid to Cian as he walked through the courtyard—as he'd heard it seemed when you finally faced the headsman's axe. The air was alive with the sharp, acidic smell of the tanning hides and sweet with the aroma of cane being boiled for its sap, overlaying the mellower aroma of baking bread. The flagstones had an indefinable extra substantiality beneath his feet, and the golden grass of the walls had never shone so brightly. Bright *edhean* was warm on the back of his neck, and it seemed to Cian Canbhei as if he could hear every single sound of the day's work: the rasp of the scrapers, the bubbling of the cane-tubs, the slap of every footstep and every word of every conversation, if only he'd wished to stop and listen.

Cianna came up to him before he reached the gate. "You're taking so little, then?" For all Cian carried with him was his knife and cloak, a bag of dried meat at his

14

belt, and a blanket wrapped into a long roll over his shoulder.

"I have all I shall remember of this place," Cian said, "and that will be enough. Otherwise, I should wish to take everything and find myself too burdened to move."

"Well, this much more shall you take with you," Cianna told him, and reached to pin a golden badge to the collar of his cloak, a Canbhei token of peaceful passage.

Cian fingered it uncertainly. "But I do not travel for the clan."

"You are Canbhei," his sister reproved him, "and we would not let you leave that behind even if you wished to. Wherever you go, you will go with the protection of our name." Then she produced a bag of coin, not substantially lighter than his food pouch. "Nor will we have you allowing people to think the Canbhei an uncharitable people."

"No, we would not want that, would we?"

"We shall not have it." Her duties as hold-lord finished, Cianna let her stern, official expression vanish and became his sister once again. "You won't be forgotten, Cian. Whenever you have found whatever you're looking for, come back to us. Your name will be remembered here."

"I will."

Dhein approached him next. "May *edhean*'s light be upon you always, Cian."

"And you, sister. I hope I learn enough of my *sgeadhanha-dan* to explain it to you one day."

"The lessons will be there, Cian. Look for them. Listen to them. There's no better counsel I might give you."

"I'd look for none better from the *an-sgeadhan* himself."

Then their arms were around him, and he returned their embrace strongly, though they respected him enough to release him quickly when he loosed his grip.

"I cannot wish *adhe*'s blessings upon you," Cianna said, "for I fear you will go beyond even her reach. But fair journey, traveler."

"To joyous endings." Dhein finished the benediction.

They didn't close the gates behind him when he went out, and when he turned to look back from the edge of the woods long minutes later, they were still open. For a turbulent instant, he was torn by a desire to rush back within those sheltering walls, but he had said that he would go forth and decided at last that it would be the first act of the Cian Canbhei he hoped to become that he kept to that oath. He turned back to the woodline and was lost to sight within the trees.

Chapter Two

Cian Canbhei met the silver giant at a fork in the narrow forest path. It was standing still as a forgotten icon in the shadowed, verdant ruins of some overgrown shrine to Cian's shattered life, where a shaft of late-afternoon sunshine pierced the low-hanging canopy of broad *aceail* leaves to lave it in molten bronze.

The young *gal-adheni* approached the giant slowly. He was not afraid, quite. He had heard of such wonders, even in the distant, insular fields of his lost family holding. But the reality of it, pure and bright as a stack of newly minted coins gleaming in coppery firelight, was nevertheless a daunting thing.

Some unknown power had anchored the giant where it stood, driving its two long legs shin deep into the softer soil beside the path. Even so imbedded, the giant still stood nearly twice Cian's stocky height. But it was slender— when Cian nerved himself to venture a touch, his hands nearly met around its waist, and he doubted it weighed even as much as he did. The flesh of the giant's body shone like the blade of the good Canbhei knife in Cian's belt, yet it yielded under his palms with the feel of softly tanned leather. For a moment, Cian's hands shamed him. They felt coarse, callous, harsh, against the thing they encircled.

The giant turned and looked at him, and it felt as though the soft metal was flowing under Cian's hands in

17

the instant before he snatched them away and retreated back beyond the giant's reach. The featureless face lifted to follow him. A single point of radiance seemed to shine out at him from someplace somehow within the surface of that perfect oval. Cian found his gaze drawn to it almost automatically and wondered if it served any other purpose.

"Fair journey, traveler," the giant said. The words flowed from unbroken silver where Cian would have looked for a mouth. The tongue was Cian's own, but the accent was like none he'd ever heard, more liquid and higher-pitched even than the speech of the soft-handed decadents of the South Coast. That the giant spoke the ritual benediction of the *breahn-adhe* was only another surprise, scarcely sufficient by then to astonish Cian any further.

"To joyous endings," he replied without hesitation, for the Canbhei were a courteous people, even in hardship, even to surprising giants.

"Yes." The giant looked down to where the coiled, springy grass grew up unbroken around its shins. "I would seem to have done, wouldn't I?" Was that laughter in its voice? Cian couldn't be sure; he didn't know how to listen to the speech of giants. "Where are you bound?"

"I seek the Consortium Enclave," said Cian Canbhei, the pain of the admission once again darkening his countenance, "with an offer of service."

"So. An adventurer," the giant said. "A seeker of novelty."

"A hireling," Cian said curtly. "A seeker of opportunity."

The giant nodded once, slowly. It seemed to Cian as if it were carefully adding up his travel-stained cloak of umber wool and the depleted sag of the food pouch at his belt, tallying them in with the thick mud caked on his boots to take the full measure of his destitution before replying.

"Taking service with the Consortium is a long path

to walk for opportunity," it said at last, too cheerfully for Cian's liking.

"Some of us have to look farther than others, giant," Cian said. He wanted to hit it, he realized irrationally. Something in the bright, ignorant way the giant flicked at the open wound of Cian's forced departure from the land Canbhei blood had nourished for as long as there had been a land made him want to take that slender neck and tie three different knots in it. "This is the path left me to follow, and so I walk it."

"Well, then," said the giant, "from here all roads lead to the Enclave, even if you had no need to go there."

"Good," Cian snapped. He stared at the fork in the path and chose the rightmost turning. It led downhill at a slight angle that would make walking easier. He started forward.

The giant's voice followed him. "Of course, some roads are better than others."

He was not going to turn back, Cian told himself. The giant had said both paths led to the Enclave. He had chosen the direction he would take. And he did not want to talk to the giant anymore. . . .

"What is so grand about that other path?" he called without turning.

"The hospitality of *adhe*," the giant answered, "for those who would accept it."

A *breahn-adhe*. That would mean warm food, which he had not tasted in a week, and a good bed, the luxury of which seemed a memory almost beyond recall. And friendly company that would accept him for a night the way he could let none of his name ever accept him again. . . .

"And what is so terrible about this path?"

"Why, nothing if you do not mind swamp mud and hungry *srithin*."

Cian Canbhei minded hungry *srithin*. He minded anything with that many teeth and that big an appetite. He turned and started back up the path to the fork, muttering a dour invocation of Creac's wrath upon smug giants and life in general. Halfway there, a stone turned beneath his foot, and he slipped, barking a knuckle and holing the knee of his heavy leggings in the process.

"Too bad," the giant sympathized. "That's nice material."

"How far is this *breahn-adhe*?" Cian demanded. Perhaps the trick was to ignore the thing's attempts at conversation. "I wish to partake of their damned hospitality."

"Perhaps fifty great-casts," the giant answered. "You should be able to reach it before the rain comes, if you hasten."

Cian looked up into the cloudless sky. The golden afternoon sunlight was warm against his face. "Do you recommend haste, giant?"

"If rain troubled me and I valued neighborly counsel, I would certainly hurry."

"Then I shall act accordingly," Cian said. He thrust his thumbs into the slack of his belt and set off easily up the left path. A small rock lay before him; he kicked it aside in casual retaliation for its offending kinsman below and to show the giant just how little he valued its advice. If the giant recognized his deliberate lack of speed, it gave no sign.

"Fair journey, traveler," it called after him.

Rust in *srith* piss, Cian thought sourly. But the Canbhei were a courteous folk.

"To joyous endings," he answered grudgingly. Surely blessed *adhe* in her wisdom didn't require you to mean it. . . .

The thunder of rain on the roof all but drowned out the pounding on the door.

Kellin Breahnin rushed to answer, hesitating only long enough to hand the steaming bowl he bore to young Berin, Sabha's oldest daughter, and shoo her in the direction of the far table. The flowing white cloth of his robe collapsed in sodden grayness the instant he opened the door and the driving storm gusted in.

Cian Canbhei glared in at the *breahn*. The force of the rain had long since overcome the natural oils of his woolen cloak, which clung to his head and shoulders like a half-shed skin. His jerkin sagged as though lined with thick mail, and his leonine beard had been reduced to a sodden tangle whose weight pulled at his chin. He resembled nothing so much as a weathered *aceail* stump shrouded in damp moss.

"Fair journey, traveler," Kellin said, somewhat ruefully, aware of the incongruity of the benediction in such a context.

"To joyous endings," Cian forced out through gritted teeth, "as long as they're dry." He squelched past the *breahn* standing in the antechamber, into the *breahn-adhe* proper. The warmth from the roaring hearth, visible through the inner arch, rolled over him in a great coddling wave; the smells of good cooking raced the babble of enthusiastic conversation for his first notice.

A soggy weight lifted from his shoulders, and he turned to see his sopping cloak staggering away atop the legs of a *breahnin* child. Cloak and child alike were immediately swallowed up in the press of the *breahn-adhe*'s company, for the storm without had driven everyone within reach of the traveler's sanctuary to seek its shelter. They clustered happily around the low, rough-hewn tables, South Coast traders, all in red and gold, intermixed with scarred, dour-handed champions in well-worn armor, their tokens of passage and challenge put aside at the door, while wide-eyed young pilgrims journeying in search of places named in half a dozen songs of heritage looked on in delighted awe. Business and history and more than one declaration of war had been placed in abeyance in accord with the fellowship of the *breahn-adhe*, which permitted no such petty considerations to intrude on the openhanded hospitality the *breahnin* professed as the purest worship of *adhe* herself. The *sgeadhanha-dan* of the place, its atmosphere of camaraderie and the community born of shared inconvenience, cut Cian to the heart, reminding him of all he had given up before it could be taken from him. It was a unit; they were a unit, and he was apart from it. His shoulders sagged, as if his sodden cloak had been draped back across them threefold. He turned to face Kellin Breahnin.

"Please forgive my discourtesy—" he began.

Kellin waved the apology aside. "Bad weather wears on good manners."

"Yet decent guesting demands them. I must apologize."

Kellin shrugged and laughed. "Then I must accept, I suppose. But I could put the breath to better use offering you dry clothing and a hot meal."

Cian smiled then. "And I mine, to accept."

The robe of heavy fur was dry and warm and clean against his skin. Cian sat back in his corner and wrapped himself deeper in its comfort. His own clothing had gone to join the masses of leather and wool and more exotic fabric on the racks laid out before the hearth, the moisture steaming out of their fibers.

Kellin Breahnin made his way back to Cian's table, a pragmatic leather apron belted over his robes, carrying a steaming wooden bowl.

"Courtesy of the Holdless Clan," he announced, setting it down before Cian. Cian couldn't answer. The smell of cooked meat and vegetables in thick simmering gravy struck him like a blow, sending a thrill of sensation through him. Spoon in hand, he stared down at the bowl almost in trepidation.

"Seven nights I have dreamed of a meal like this," he said, breaking the end from a fresh, soft loaf of bread and dipping it almost reverently into black-brown gravy, "and woke up to dried meat and foraged *bhan* nuts. . . ."

"The benevolence of *adhe* is a blessing wherever it is found."

"Well, yes, to be sure," Cian said quickly. "But when it's *cooked*—"

"And so in our small way may we enhance her bounty. Your appreciation is appreciated in turn. What good fortune brings you past our gates?"

"A wonder."

"Truly?"

"Indeed. A silver giant that counseled me, rather annoyingly, to follow this path—" Kellin Breahnin was smiling ruefully and shaking his head. "What did I say?"

"I would not have thought him still there after all this time."

"You know of him?"

"And well I should," Kellin Breahnin said. "I put him there."

"Truly? Another wonder, then. And how did you come to undertake such a task?"

"Well, he was mine, after all."

"You own a silver giant?" Cian was reminded again that he was a long way from any land he knew and understood. "Is that common among the *breahnin*?"

"Not if my word carries any weight," Kellin said with feeling. "It was a gift, you see, from the factor of the Consortium Enclave."

"Creatures of the Enclave come here?"

"It is not a far journey, even for *gal-adheni* afoot. And it is no distance at all for the conveyances of the Enclave. We see them often enough; they are curious about us. The giant was presented to us as a courtesy, a 'servant to the servants,' they called it."

"The Holdless Clan is no one's servant, surely."

"I never said they understood us," Kellin answered. "But the gift was well-meant, and we took no offense."

"Then why set it out upon the road?"

"Because it was too rich a gift," Kellin said, "and too fine a servant. It left us nothing to do; it tended to our guests so thoroughly that I feared we risked becoming the hands of *adhe* in name only. And besides, as I believe

23

you noticed, that constant, infernal cheerfulness was maddening."

"And so you stuck it into a hillside."

"Where it might at least direct travelers to us and where *I* didn't have to listen to it," Kellin said. "Just so."

"Very wise."

"One tries. And because one tries, I ask again: what brought you past our gates?"

"Did I not tell you?"

"No. You told me how you found us, not how you came to be traveling where we might be found."

"Must I give an accounting of myself, then?"

"Don't glower so! The hospitality of *adhe* is offered freely to all who would accept it. It is merely to satisfy my own curiosity that I ask. But one of the rewards of our calling is meeting travelers and thus partaking of the entire world in the comfort of our own halls. I offer no compulsion."

"Then I must apologize again for my discourtesy. I follow this road because I seek the Consortium Enclave myself, with an offer of service."

Kellin Breahnin nodded. "I thought as much. What could drive you to make such an offer? You are young yet, and the Canbhei are an honorable clan and prosperous. Why should you wish to leave?"

"I do not wish to leave," Cian said. "Creac's eyes, I wish it was not needful. But I cannot stay. There is nothing for me among my own people any longer."

"Why not?"

"Because I have committed the one crime against them for which there is no atoning."

"And what is that?" Kellin asked quietly, for there were some trespasses that forfeited even the hospitality of *adhe*.

"I was born too late," said Cian Canbhei.

"*Ai,*" said Kellin Breahnin, realizing. "*Ai, shta.*"

"Fen Canbhei was a great hold-lord and a good steward. He widened out lands every year for twenty years; he increased the harvests from those lands every season. His *sgeadhanha-dan* was a vigorous one. The an-Canbhei himself could not boast one better. But"—Cian spread his hands helplessly—"may *adhe* harbor my father's bones in comfort, but he never knew when enough was enough."

"How many children?"

"Three, two daughters and myself."

"Not excessive, surely."

"Two too many for the good of the clan. There can be only one heir. One. And I am not it."

"And so they are casting you out?"

"No!" Cian said quickly. "No, never. The Canbhei do not turn on their own. But—what would there be for me among them? Cianna is hold-lord now, and she deserves the title; she has prepared for it from childhood. Dhein is content with her studies; she will be a formidable *sgeadhan* someday. But what am I to do? Shall I just wait, hovering in the shadows, peering over Cianna's shoulder. 'Hello, sister. Are you well, sister? Do you think you might die soon, sister?' I could not live so."

"I cannot believe that a Canbhei would behave in such a fashion."

"Nor would I. But if I can conceive of it now, might I not come to live it, given enough time? I am not prepared to risk that. So it is plain that I must seek my future elsewhere."

"But with the Consortium, the Basiri? To divorce yourself from the flesh of *adhe* herself? If you must leave your hold, you must; this is not the first time such a thing has happened, and I do not say you are not wise to seek to make your own way. But service with the Consortium is so—permanent. If you must take service outside your clan, then why not turn at least to others of our own kind?"

"Because the Canbhei are not servants any more than are the Holdless Clan. A Canbhei in service with another clan is a Canbhei who failed, who could not live up to his name. I will not do that to my family. But the

25

Consortium, what is the Consortium? A dome in a field, unlikely stories told over too much *bhan-sir*; it isn't the same, somehow. It isn't quite real, do you see, if only because it is so far away, and I would not have to bear my shame in front of anyone who mattered. And when I come back, then perhaps I will have the means to found a holding of my own."

"And if you do not come back? Many have not."

"Then my failure will not befoul the *sgeadhanhadan* of the Canbhei."

"No," Kellin agreed. "It would not. Nor would you be alive to know it."

"Just as well. Creac's shield needs many bearers. This excellent food is growing cold, I fear. I thank you for putting up with my tawdry little story, *Breahn*—"

"A service of the house. You wanted to talk."

"I needed to talk, rather—and you saw it before I did. But now I believe I would assay this fine meal and turn my thoughts to my first meeting with my prospective employers."

Kellin Breahnin turned at the sound of the outer door's opening and then looked back at him. "You won't have to think about it for long."

It might have been the giant's sister, a slender silver statuette framed in the timber archway of the hall. Then it moved, and the light of the hearth-fire reached within the folds of the loose hood to reveal the creature of flesh beneath the artifice.

"Is that a Basiri, then?" Cian asked, never taking his gaze from the advancing creature.

"That is a garment such as they wear," Kellin Breahnin said. "They are frail, you know, and claim to need such robes to bear the embrace of *adhe*. But this one is slight even for a Basiri, and I have never seen one with such eyes—but I forget my responsibilities. Please excuse me."

Dani Yuen looked down over the heads of the natives gathered, staring curiously around her as the bustling, incredibly stocky individual scattered her audience like chaff, breasting the crowd to reach her.

He came to an abrupt halt before her, a squat boulder of flesh and bone shrouded in white and crowned with a mane of coarse black hair shot through liberally with white. His short, stumping stride and the energetic vigor with which he shepherded his gawking charges into order reminded Dani of the one other of his kind she had known. She remembered the price that other had paid for that vigor, along with the further coin she had journeyed past all human frontiers to exact.

"*Ayanim*, your pardons, please! Allow our new guest to come in out of the rain! Sabha, Trelan, *breahnin*, shame! A traveler seeks our hospitality, and you stand there, gaping! Berin would know better, and she scarce old enough to serve at all! My humblest apologies, *ayan*"—and only here did Kellin's decision desert him—"*aya*—?"

Dani rescued him quickly, summoning the feminine honorific up from her limited knowledge of *gal-adheni* vocabulary.

"*Aya, breahn*," she said. "*Aya* Dani Yuen, of Earth and farther places."

"*Aya*, Yuen. Please excuse my ignorance."

"There is nothing to excuse, *breahn*. There was no reason you should know."

"Your forebearance is appreciated. But I fear my dotage overtakes me when I can no longer tell man from woman, even among strangers."

"How strange. Among my people, the older a man gets, the more excessively aware he seems to become of the presence of young women."

Kellin laughed. "Then perhaps we are not so different at that, for all your height, *aya*. But forgive me again. I reproach my own for keeping you standing and then repeat their sin. Come this way, please. Are you alone?"

"Oh, yes. Quite alone, *breahn*."

27

"Would you care for a seat near to the hearth, perhaps, to take away the chill of traveling?"

"I did not come by foot. I am quite comfortable, thank you."

"Then would you honor us by accepting the bounty of *adhe*—your pardon again, *aya*, but is our food acceptable to you?"

"From what they told me at the Enclave, I will take no harm from it"—it was her turn to pause, to rake her memory for the correct protocol—"and the honor lies in accepting *adhe*'s bounty. It has been a long day for me, *breahn*, and I should like very much to be honored."

"By all means." Kellin Breahnin paused to scan the crowded hall, seeking an open table. He looked into the dark corner of the room, and Cian Canbhei was looking back, black eyes bright with firelight and curiosity. Kellin turned back to the Earthwoman. "This way, *aya*."

The young *gal-adheni* sitting alone at the corner table rose as Kellin Breahnin led Dani over. Palms flat on the table top, he still could not entirely straighten the thick, hugely muscled arms that would reach down almost to his knees as he stood.

"Cian Fen-sired, of Canbhei named, would you offer the hospitality of *adhe* to *Aya* Yuen of Earth?"

"The blessing of *adhe* is born of acceptance," Cian answered formally. "Would the Yuen so honor me?"

"Gladly," Dani said, sitting.

A *gal-adheni* stool was far too short-legged for human comfort; she would have had to sit with her knees drawn up into her chest. But *gal-adheni* were built low and built wide, shaped by a world's gravity twice that Dani Yuen had been born to; she could have stood beside herself before the alien who offered her his table and not cleared the span of his shoulders. She was able to draw her legs up on the broad seat of the stool with ease, gathering the folds of her robe of Consortium gravitic mesh beneath her.

She had to be the most fragile creature Cian Canbhei had ever seen. He had thought the silver giant

28

slender, but it had been power and strength personified by comparison. How could that slender column of a neck possibly support the weight of her head, Cian wondered. The thin hands she clasped on the table—and what mad god had ever thought so many fingers necessary?—looked smaller than a child's against the utensils and bowl there. Even her long, fine black hair seemed as though it should have been hopelessly crushed by the weight of the hood that contained it.

"A Yuen of Earth, then," said Cian Canbhei. "So you are not Basiri. Yet you are much as I imagined them, *aya*."

"Not really," Dani said. "They're just about as much taller again as I am to you—from what little of them I've seen. I've never met one up close."

"But surely you must have, *aya*. Only Consortium ships ever call here."

Dani shook her head, wondering if the gesture translated. The Consortium mnemonic tape she had taken covered language and customs well enough, but she would not rely on it for nuance. Too often, not even the best translators between species knew what to look for.

"I didn't have twenty years to spare taking passage on a City Mercantile, so I came in on a Jirin stitch-ship—" She recognized Cian's puzzled stare. "I'm sorry. You have no idea what I'm talking about, do you? I didn't realize."

"It's not exactly everyday knowledge for us, usually. But I look forward to learning."

"Oh. Well, Basiri live a long time—"

"How long?"

Dani could only shrug. "They don't offer many specifics. Some people think as long as they care to. But however long it is, they can take their time between ports of call, and they don't trouble themselves to fit their schedules to anyone who might be in more of a hurry."

"So you chose to travel by a stitch-ship, whatever that is."

"That's the star-drive pattern the Jirin use. It's faster than a City Mercantile, as long as you don't mind living with two-legged snakes for a few months."

"I think I might."

"Their table manners do leave something to be desired. Is this what you looked forward to learning?"

"I have no idea what to look forward to," Cian said. "I only feel I should learn all I can about the Consortium before I approach them."

"Approach them? Why?" And so Cian Canbhei sighed and repeated his story for the slender alien who faced him.

By the time he had finished, she had thrown back her hood to do him the courtesy of showing herself clearly while he spoke. The slim hands were folded now under her chin as she watched him.

"Kellin Breahnin was right, you know. Service with the Consortium is rather permanent."

"At twenty years' time between ports of call, he was not lying. Still, that would at least guarantee my resolve would not weaken once I took their service if I found it not to my liking. At least I should be spared the risk of that disgrace."

"Don't count on that," Dani Yuen said quietly.

"And why not?" asked Cian Canbhei.

"You're talking about choosing service with the Consortium as being preferable to the disgrace you think you risk with your own kind, right?" Cian nodded. "But have you considered the disgrace you risk out in the Consortium?"

"I don't risk disgrace in Basiri service," Cian said. "By the compact between our peoples, service to the Consortium is as honorable as service to any clan."

"I know that. But how do you define that honorable service?"

"I don't have to define it. I simply have to go to considerable trouble to perform it."

"I don't think you realize just how much trouble you might have to go to," Dani Yuen said.

There was one thing about her that belied his first impression of alien frailty, Cian realized. Her eyes were as black and alive as any *gal-adheni's*; under her stare, he suddenly became aware of her *sgeadhanha-dan* as a harder and more opaque thing than he would ever have expected. And although he reminded himself that he could not know how to read the *sgeadhanha-dan* of a creature not born of *adhe*, he felt in it an anger he could only assume was directed at himself.

"Perhaps you are right," he said. "But perhaps I don't care how much trouble I have to go through. I have left my hold, and I will leave *adhe* herself because I must, because service with the Consortium is the last proper choice left me. As to the honor of it, I'm certain I shall recognize it when I see it. I have little else to look for."

"If it's there to be recognized."

"It's there. No *gal-adheni* could be bound by the Compact if it wasn't."

"I know how *gal-adheni* keep the Compact," said Dani Yuen. "But how do you know anyone else does?"

"Will you tell me they do not? How could that be? How could *gal-adheni* or Basiri or these Jirin you speak of—or even a Yuen of Earth—exist if they did not deal with one another honorably?"

"Not very well," Dani said. "As they don't, often enough."

"Often enough is not always," Cian said. "Anyone can fail. But the ideal, the goal of honorable conduct, is still there."

"Is it really? Do you really expect Basiri or Jirin or even Earthmen to conduct themselves like honorable little *gal-adheni?*"

"I said nothing of the sort. I'm not quite provincial enough to expect others to live up to our standards. But that does not mean that I cannot deal with them honorably. My honor is something I owe to myself, not

31

to others. Or is that too provincial a concept for such cosmopolitan travelers as yourself, as well?"

"Don't flatter yourself that *gal-adheni* have a monopoly on virtue," Dani said coldly. "I am as closely bound by ties of hearth-sharing and blood-swearing as any of you." Which was not quite the case, but it was the closest analogue she could find in the mnemonic for her own unbreakable vow of service. "But don't assume the price of your honorable service to the Consortium is one you'll be eager, or even willing, to pay."

"I assume nothing," Cian answered, "but my own certainty that I am capable of loyal service to *any* honorable master." He fought to control his temper. "*Aya*, forgive me; I invite you to share my table and then offer you my anger in place of courtesy. I must ask your pardon."

Dani matched his restraint. "Bad temper seems to be served in equal portions around here. I take no offense. But perhaps we might restrict ourselves to more congenial topics. . . ."

"So you have traveled among the worlds of the Consortium?"

"Between them would be a more honest description," Dani corrected him. "Traveling between worlds is not the same as following a road from one clan-hold to the next."

"I should think it was a bit far to walk."

"The distance you have to travel isn't the problem. It's the way you have to travel that distance. You decide you want to leave a world. So you book passage aboard a Terran starliner, or a Consortium City Mercantile—or a Jirin stitch-ship, if that's what's on hand." Dani grimaced. "A starliner's fine; we humans like our comfort. And a City Mercantile makes a starliner look about as sophisticated as this table. But stitch-ships—well, you have to like food that kicks when you fork it. Jirin are funny that way."

"I'll have to remember to laugh."

"But that isn't the problem either."

"No?"

"No. The trouble with traveling between worlds is that you don't go anyplace."

Cian put his tankard down slowly. "You're going to explain that, I trust."

"All you do when you board a starship is climb into a box, and stay there just long enough to get bored, no matter how comfortable the box is. There's no sense of actually going anyplace."

"Now how can that be?" Cian demanded. "I've never traveled aboard a starship, but I've traveled enough in waterborne craft to know when they're moving, even when I'm belowdecks."

"It isn't the same," Dani said. "A seagoing ship is *part* of its environment. The water works on it, the wind works on it, and you can tell you're moving by observing this. But a spaceship is designed to keep you as completely segregated from the environment you're traveling through as it possibly can. You have no real referents to prove you've moving.

"And then, after you've become good and bored with the unchanging routine of your traveling box, you climb out of it in someplace completely different from where you got in—and everything you know is wrong. You don't know the languages, you don't know the customs, you don't know the local mores, you don't know the people and sometimes you *can't* know them. And the worst thing of all is that you've had no time to adjust to these differences. It's not as if you've been walking along a road, watching things change, seeing the differences grow. They're simply there, just like that—and there's no way to get back to anything you consider normal, nowhere to get away from the two-legged snakes and food that screams when you eat it."

"You've made your point," Cian said. "I'll make sure to avoid the Jirin."

Dani exhaled wearily. "No. You've missed my point.

At least with the Jirin you can see the differences right off. With most of us, you'd never be so lucky. . . ."

The courtyard of the breahn-adhe smelled of cooking and damp grass the morning after the rain. Cian had slept little, for he and the Yuen had stayed up until the hearth was but glowing embers, exchanging stories, he of life in the embrace of *adhe*, she of a universe in which he still did not entirely believe. He wondered how much, if any, of what she had told him the night before had been pure fabrication, and how much nightmare misremembered.

Kellin Breahnin was overseeing a gaggle of *breahnin* children as they industriously swept the puddles from the cobbled courtyard. The door behind him opened, and Dani Yuen emerged, shrouded in her shimmering robe.

The morning sun was bright and warm, and Cian had rolled his cloak, freshly oiled by Kellin himself, into a bundle he could sling from one shoulder. The *breahn* looked up and grinned as he saw Cian approaching.

"Blessings to *adhe* for this glorious morning, young friend," he called. "And will you be leaving us so soon?"

"There seems no point to putting it off," Cian answered. "If I have to travel, I may as well get where I'm going."

"Then fair journey, traveler," intoned Kellin Breahnin.

"To joyous endings."

Dani Yuen smiled politely as he approached her. "I am no child of *adhe*," she said, "and so it would be presumptuous of me to offer you her blessings. But I wish you good fortune."

Cian nodded politely. "And I you, *Aya*."

He paused at the shrine before the *breahn-adhe* gate. The *breahnin* made no demands for the service they provided, and most travelers were content to leave what they felt to be a fair return for their food and lodgings, generally a few silver pieces. But if a traveler was not well set up, a few bronzes or even a written benediction were accepted with equal grace. Cian hefted his change purse thoughtfully. He was by no means poor, for his sisters had been generous in equipping him for his travels—but he doubted *galadheni* coin would be of any use to him where he traveled next. The pouch clinked heavily as he set it down on the altar and walked on by into the road, toward the morning sun and the thin scrim of clouds along the horizon.

Did it do nothing but rain in these damned hills?

Cian trudged along sullenly under the weight of his newly soaked cloak. The thin line of clouds along the morning horizon had swept overhead and thickened into a proper thunderstorm in a matter of hours. The trail had turned to mud and loose stones beneath him, and more than once he had slipped and fallen. The sloppy trail slowed his progress; already it was dark, and he doubted he was more than halfway to the Consortium Enclave.

The continued downpour chilled him deeply, and this time as he walked, he did not have the strengthening knowledge of shelter ahead, for there was no other *breahn-adhe* between himself and the Enclave, and it was a part of the hills few chose to live in. Few folk wanted the Enclave for neighbors.

He trudged onward. His feet were wet and swollen, and his tunic stuck to his back like oil. Water dripping from the peak of his hood soaked his beard and trickled down onto his chest, and if he pulled his hood far enough forward to stop the dripping, he couldn't see where he was going and fell flat on his face every few steps.

Dani watched his progress dispassionately as the rain swirled and blurred the view through the bubble canopy of her Consortium flyer. The storm and the intervening trees offered no obstacle to the Basiri-made scanner pickups; she could follow Cian's every stumbling step in comfort and convenience.

She had to admire his certainty; it was a rare quality

35

in the more refined reaches of the Consortium Mercantile and her own Terran Confederacy that she was used to. And it figured, she thought bitterly, that she should end up in just such a backwater as this before she could hope to regain her own.

Silent in its alien sophistication, indifferent to the buffeting of wind and storm, her flyer drifted slowly above the toiling *gal-adheni*, pursuing him to a destination Dani counted on Cian to find for her.

He was wet and miserable and discouraged, and when he saw the light upon the hillside, he didn't even register it at first.

Then it did register, warm firelight shining beacon-like through a roughly framed window in a crude stone hut perhaps a single cast uphill of the trail. A narrow pathway, steep and rocky, led up to the hut.

Cian debated making the climb. Anyone who lived that far out in the middle of nowhere must prize their privacy even more so than most *gal-adheni*. For an ungrateful, unworthy second, he regretted leaving the whole of his coin to the *breahn-adhe*, for such a hermit as must live above him was in no way under the same obligation of hospitality the *breahnin* set themselves.

"Why don't you go up, child?"

The speaker might have been a part of the landscape, just another rain-beaten boulder, so still did he stand as Cian whirled to face him. It was impossible in the darkness to make out any face within the shadows of his dripping cloak, impossible to observe any detail save the cocked and loaded crossbow the stranger aimed at him one-handed, steadied against a long leather sling wrapped around his neck.

"It's rare enough that I get a visitor," Cian's captor said. "Go on up, then."

The rain-slick stones of the path were treacherous; more than one rock turned beneath Cian's foot or barked his shin in the dark. But the stranger followed him with sure feet and a steady pace, climbing with practiced familiarity. Cian saw that he made no effort to keep up with his reluctant visitor—after all, there was no place Cian could run on the exposed hillside that a crossbow quarrel could not reach faster.

The loose hide flap that served as the hut's only door dangled and flapped in the gusting storm winds. Cian pulled the flap aside, and then, at a gesture from the armed stranger, flung it up over the low roof of the hut, leaving the doorway unobstructed.

His initial sensation of overwhelming warmth almost blotted out Cian's alarm, for the fire pit in the center of the hut was fully stoked and blazing, venting through the smoke-hole at the peak of the hut's roof.

The bowman came through the doorway behind him, and Cian retreated to the far side of the fire pit at quarrel's point.

"There's no sense to your getting my good dirt floor all muddy," he said. "Get that cloak off before you drown in your own puddle. Over there," he added, pointing Cian's path with the weapon.

The wall to which he directed the young *gal-adheni* was lined with pegs and hooks hammered between the uneven stones that made up the hut, fixed in the clay caulking. A drainage gutter lined with gravel ran along the base of the wall, through a gap between the stones, and downhill. Cian shrugged out of his cloak and, after a moment's hesitation, his tunic, hanging them up and turning to examine his surroundings. There was a rough table, a stool, a pallet for sleeping, a crude iron frame erected over the fire-pit from which a fire-scored pot swung. The walls were hung with smoked cuts of meat and *dhenil* cheeses. Boxes of various sizes around the walls held clothing and blankets and tools.

But there were a number of items that Cian didn't recognize. The edge of the table was lined with an odd collection of blocks and spikes, whose like he had not seen before.

Cian looked back to the stranger, who had stood patiently while Cian stripped out of his wet garments.

Behind him, the unbarred doorway stood open and tempting, even with the rain gusting in.

"Should I get the door, then?" Cian asked.

The stranger laughed shortly. "It will get itself, easily enough."

Almost as he spoke, a particularly fierce gust brought the hide flapping and flailing down off the roof, to fill the doorway. "But you may make it fast, if you like. No sense in letting all that good heat go to waste."

Moving as slowly as if performing a stately caracole, they circled the fire until Cian was beside the doorway. The hide, he saw, secured to small hooks in the door frame with simple looped thongs—and the crossbow, he saw, still centered on him. He rather doubted he could move his entire body through the door and beyond faster than his imposed host could move his finger the length of a trigger-pull. He set himself to fastening the loops, securing the hide against the wind.

The stranger relaxed once the task was done and the doorway was blocked by the thick skin.

"Good, then," he said. "Excuse me a moment."

His eyes never left Cian as he set the crossbow down on the table top, still cocked. He reached up with the hand thus freed and undid the collar of his cloak, and Cian saw the reason for his odd style of marksmanship.

His right arm was gone, missing entirely from the shoulder down. With his left hand, he tossed the cloak across the fire-pit to Cian.

"If you would be so kind," he said, and Cian shrugged and set the cloak on a peg beside his own. The stranger grinned at him, lopsidedly, where the patches of scar tissue from old burns would still let his face move. He rubbed at his ruined shoulder. "A remembrance for old services rendered," he said. He pulled a joint of meat from a hook above the table, and Cian saw the reason for the spikes. The stranger slapped the meat down atop them, impaling it in place, and then picked up a knife and began to slice it up one-handed with meticulous care, although he never became so engrossed in the task that he failed to notice when Cian tried to move toward him and laid a warning hand on the stock of his crossbow.

"Don't try that," he suggested good-naturedly. "We've been getting along so well, so far. Relax, child." His continued references to Cian's youth puzzled Cian, even as they began to annoy him, for although it was difficult to tell with the distortion of the scars, the stranger seemed little older than himself, even though his hair and beard were liberally streaked with gray.

"This is surely the most peculiar waylaying I have ever heard of," Cian said.

"Waylaying?" The stranger sounded wounded. "Nothing of the kind. I merely offered you shelter from the storm and the chance of a hot meal. I judged you would welcome it."

"Are you in the habit conveying your invitations by force of arms, then?"

"It seemed advisable. Travelers to the Enclave are often unnecessarily excitable."

"How did you know I seek the Enclave?"

"No one ever follows this path for any other reason. Besides, would you deny it?"

"I have done nothing I would conceal from anyone."

"Well, good for you, child. Would you?" He indicated the meat on the table and backed away with his weapon as Cian came and placed it in the pot over the fire. But he did not trouble to hold the point on Cian anymore, as though he assumed some unspoken agreement between them had rendered it unnecessary. He set himself on the edge of a crate, the crossbow across his knees, watching his guest and the bubbling pot.

Cian took the stool near the table and sat himself.

"Even kidnappers usually have names," he said.

"As do their victims—guests, rather," the stranger pointed out.

"I am Cian Fen-sired, of Canbhei named," Cian said. "And yourself?"

"Óin," the other said, the mask of his good humor evaporating.

"Óin what?"

"Óin," the stranger repeated, with a sharp note of finality. And then Cian understood.

"*Aidjiin!*" he exclaimed, and shot to his feet as though the stool beneath him had grown horns. "Creac take your black soul!" He quickly snatched down his sodden tunic and began to struggle into it.

"What in *adhe*'s name do you think you're doing?" Óin asked.

"A Canbhei does not associate with outlaws," Cian snapped, "even under duress!" He pulled down his cloak and took two steps toward the door before he found himself staring at the gleaming black iron point of Óin's quarrel again.

"Well, good for you, child," Óin said. "Of course it seems to me such a petty point to die over." Cian's hand was wrapped tightly around the hilt of his long knife, half-drawn from the scabbard he had never removed.

"You won't get from there to here, child," Óin warned him.

"Then what do you suggest, *aidjiin?*"

Óin grinned. "I suggest that there's no such thing as outlaw stew and that it probably wouldn't corrupt even such a virtuous child as yourself to eat a hot meal in the company of a nameless outcast. Now sit down."

Cian hesitated. The choice between swallowing his pride along with a hot meal or trying to digest a crossbow bolt was not a difficult one.

"I suppose it won't hurt."

"Only if you don't like rock peppers."

Cian sat sullenly with his back to a wall, watching his *aidjiin* host eat. Óin had set his bowl between two large, curved blocks on the table, that held it in place while he spooned out meat and vegetables.

"Feel depraved and disgraced yet?" Óin asked.

"Not as yet," Cian said grudgingly.

"Good. It's the rock peppers, you know. Plenty of virtue in rock peppers." He laughed shortly. "What in Creac's name are you seeking out the Consortium for, child, if you don't want to meet distasteful strangers?"

"As distasteful as *aidjiin*, do you mean?"

"Count yourself fortunate if *aidjiin* are the worst you meet."

"Why should I take the word of an *aidjiin* for that?"

"Creac only knows. But if you're stupid enough to take service with the Consortium, perhaps you'll be stupid enough to listen to me."

"Taking service with the Consortium is something I have to do," said Cian Canbhei. "Your advice I don't have to tolerate."

"It's something you have to do, is it? Hope to get something out of it, do you?"

"Yes, I do."

"Such as what?"

"Nothing you'd appreciate, *aidjiin*."

"Ah, honor, then, and fame and maybe even enough wealth to start a holding of your own, is that it? Am I right?"

"What does it matter to you?"

"Now? Not a thing, not at all. But I wanted all those things once myself before I walked this path."

"You've served the Consortium?"

"Oh, yes, child, I served the Consortium. In fact, that service made me what I am today. And shall I show you what you'll get from them, child?" He twitched his empty shoulder peculiarly.

"What are you doing?"

"Wriggling my fingers, if I had any there! That's what you'll get out of the Consortium, if you're lucky. A stump and a hovel on a hillside and some black, black memories. Give it up, child."

"I don't believe you."

"I'm not surprised. They never do, at first."

"They?"

"You. All you children, wandering past here looking

41

for the Enclave and some magic pathway to your fortunes. What makes you so wonderful, child, what makes any of you so wonderful, that you'll do any better than I did?"

"I'm a warrior, trained and bred. I've mastered the Five Lines of Attack and the Three Circles of Warding—"

"A warrior, eh? With that?" He pointed at the knife in Cian's belt. "A Canbhei cane-knife, is it? How long is that?"

"Two and a half spans."

"Two and a half spans. You can face somebody two and a half spans away in fair combat. Did you ever hear of a Kors arcer, child? You know what it does? A Kors arcer throws lightning, child, kills with thunder, it does, and do you know how far it can kill? Ten great-casts, if you can aim it that well. It will kill anything you can hit, ten great-casts away. And do you know what? You can hold a Kors arcer in the palm of your hand. So don't talk to me about being a warrior, child, or I'll tell you about some of the Consortium's *real* weapons, and then I'll have to sit up all night listening to you scream. What else do you have that makes you worth a damn?"

"I have a name," Cian said hotly, "which is more than some of us can say!"

Óin sobered. "Yes, child, you have a name, and you have your unbreakable *gal-adheni* honor and your pride, don't you? Well, I had a name once, and I was just as stiff-backed and honorable as you are, and there was a time when I could afford pride, yes, even an *aidjiin*, even me. . . . And I left them all behind me, in the service of the Consortium. Do you want to know how I did that?"

"No," said Cian Canbhei.

"Well, too bad. I've nothing better to do with my life than keep you children from making the mistake I made, and by Creac's ears, you'll listen to my story if I have to hold you at quarrel's point for the whole telling of it. . . ."

* * *

Dani saw Óin rise up out of the rocks before Cian did. Her borrowed Consortium machine's keen artificial senses were not travel-weary and hampered by the storm. She witnessed the confrontation, saw Cian driven up the narrow pathway to the tumble-down hut, saw Óin follow. Then she turned to her controls and began to seek a safe place to put the flyer down.

It had been a tenuous lead at best, the stories that circulated through travelers to the Enclave of an outcast who obstructed those who came in search of service with the Consortium, seeking to turn them from their courses. She had not met any of the people this madman was alleged to have faced, for of those who did not heed his warnings and came onward, all had left their world in service to one City Mercantile or another. But it had been her best lead, made more likely by her own knowledge of the *gal-adheni* she sought. So she had located another who came to the Consortium and followed him, using him to reveal her quarry to her.

And now she had found Óin Ceiragh. . . .

Chapter Three

It was the perfect sort of crowd to be alone and far from home in.

It was Symmetry Fair on Wolkenheim, and the great binary worlds Trollshulm and Hansenwald had banished darkness from the night sky. Greedy little cargo lighters and fat intrasystem freighters pierced the sky on lances of rubied light or drifted gently into sheltering cradles on atmospheric drives. Normally staid farm folk poured into Hansen's landing from the outlying agrarian districts, shedding drab, practical workclothes for homemade costumes as outlandish and unique as possible. Raghags and buffoons, jesters and crepe-paper harlots, they all thronged the streets for the once-in-a-decade celebration of Symmetry, partying and carousing and gaping at the off-worlders in their midst. There were grim, weathered Trollshulm dragonskinners, reptilian Jirin traders, and patrician Basiri merchants from the Consortium Mercantile, among others.

One other:

Óin Ceiragh stumped through the Fair-packed streets, squat and massive, half-drunk and defiantly lonely. An ornate, freehand *breda* pipe jutted out of his thick beard, leaving thick clouds of the pungent, mildly narcotic smoke in his wake. He walked with a broad, rolling gait, clenching his fists and swinging his arms like a seaman from some older and infinitely smaller ocean

44

than the one he reluctantly navigated. It was the only way he could walk on such a world without bounding into the air at every step.

It had been a singularly unsatisfying shore leave in spite of the fact that it was Symmetry Fair.

Wolkenheim was a young world, a frontier world on the border between the brawling, outreaching Terran Confederacy and the vast Consortium Mercantile of the arrogant, enigmatic Basiri and their uncounted client/customer races, and Hansen's Landing was a port city where anyone was supposed to be able to have a good time. There was celebration and laughter all around but none for him. It was all for the great swarms of tall, fragile *humans* surrounding him, for all those creatures there on familiar, native ground, not for some strange, alien beast like a *gal-adheni*—a *gal-adheni Dwarf*, he reminded himself sourly, for if he could take Basiri coin, then he might as well accept their condescending name for their underlings—like Óin Ceiragh, so many light-years, so incredibly far from his own proper place. Among these frail creatures, born and raised in their feeble Terran-standard gravity, the strength that had been his constant and unremarkable companion in the forests and clanholds of home and his most marketable commodity in the Consortium Mercantile became a terrible and potent thing, too dangerous to let Óin enjoy the random pleasures of inebriated release.

What could he do among these delicate creatures? Could he take part in the great dances that took up whole blocks of the Fair streets? He tried, but his inhumanly quick, springy movements had looked so incongruous amid their comparatively languid and flabby undulations that dances that had been going on, unbroken, for hours collapsed as the dancers stopped to watch and mock him. Even the street bands faltered and lost their rhythms in their laughter.

Could he drink in their taverns? Seasoned innkeepers, who understood nothing of proper *breahnin* courtesy, would take one look at his man and a half's

45

shoulders and the thick traceries of tendons on his plate-sized hands and sell him anything he wanted, as long as he drank it somewhere else.

He couldn't blame them. He remembered the human whore he had visited on leaving the lighter docks. He remembered how skittish she had been around his four hundred pounds' weight. And he remembered the high, thin scream of the house's badger man when Óin had tried to backhand the human aside and wound up crushing his hip instead. He remembered the way the bones had felt, splintering under his fist.

That ended up costing him more than the badger man's rakeoff would have come to, but it had been worth it. It had impressed upon him the vulnerability of these creatures, and it served as a reminder of his ultimate alienness that he should not lose in a besotted fog.

Overhead, if he'd cared to look again, he could have seen a bright pinpoint of light, no natural satellite. That was his home and honorable employer, the star-spanning City Mercantile *Shtotha*, hanging there in the purple twilight produced by the binary worlds. That pinpoint was a reminder, too, a reminder that he could cut his leave short any time he wished and return to the routine of his service to the Basiri. But he didn't want to go back early. With six years still on his contract, he'd already had more than his fill of the pale-blooded Basiri and their muted, refined ways. He was tired of "living," to abuse the word, in quarters of metal and plastic instead of good, honest stone. He was tired of fighting for someone else's profit, even if it was the only way he would ever obtain the means to lead a proud and honorable life back home upon his unlikely return. In the meantime, he meant to enjoy any diversion he could find, no matter how depressing. But he couldn't drink in the bars, or dance in the streets, or sleep with the whores, or even find release in a good, strenuous brawl.

That left the woman.

Purely as an exercise in aesthetic appreciation, of course. In point of fact, he found little to like in most of the women of the Consortium and the Terran Confederacy. Basiri of either sex were already well enough convinced of their own superior qualities not to suffer for want of Óin's small portion of admiration, while human boldness of personality and directness grated on his clannish regard for the correct protocols of acquaintance. He found human women artless, almost crass, in comparison with the refined and civil manner of *gal-adheni* women.

The only problem with that was that the nearest *gal-adheni* woman doubtless still returned the embrace of *adhe*, however many impassable light-years away that was.

In the meantime, this woman—this girl, for he could not bring himself to think of anything so slight as a woman—was of the most common Terran or late period T-colonial stock, perhaps a foot taller than Óin, with a matte-tan complexion and straight black hair that hung loose and flowing down her back. She moved well for a human, if not with Óin's bouncy contempt for the feeble T-standard gravity, then certainly in a most amiable accommodation with it.

Óin followed the girl and her escort through the crowd, mildly interested. It wasn't the same as having a proper *gal-adheni* woman to admire, of course. Still, the hair was the right color and worn unbound, in proper fashion, and the skin color was almost right, if somewhat pale yet, and the Chinese-collared tunic and culottes she wore reminded him more than a little of the women's modest clothing back home—

"Goddammit," she said. "We lost him."

"Or he lost us," Den Ryan agreed.

They paused by a sweetmeats vendor outside a *chorst* palace, and Dani Yuen absently accepted the bag of candies Ryan handed her. They looked for all the world like two footsore tourists stopping to enjoy the sights around them rather than what they truly were: two professionals waiting for a third to try to kill them.

Dani studied the crowd passing them. She saw gaudy Fair costumes and the iridescent leathers of dragonskinners and Basiri merchants in their skullcaps and pale blue robes. Nowhere could she see the flat off-white of symbioplast armor.

"He must have cammed," she said. The light didn't help. On top of the tarnished-brass "daylight" cast by the combined binaries, the walls of the city's buildings had been adorned with an astonishing variety of lights and luminescent paints. Some of it had been strung up or brushed on in intricate combinations, meticulously planned, but more, most of it, in fact, had simply been slapped up at random to see what effect the changing natural light would produce. Nothing was the color it should have been.

Den Ryan, the taller of them, with an atavistic Nordic cast to his complexion, took advantage of his two meters' height to search the faces around him. He saw a jumbled mosaic of masks and makeup, broken occasionally by aquiline Basiri features or an excitingly brief glimpse of scales or chitin. Nowhere could he see the featureless mask of a symbioplast visor.

"Why would he bother?" he asked.

"Maybe he doesn't want any official attention."

"Then Guild White would be his best bet," Ryan argued. "What outworld constable is going to mess in Guild business?"

"Mmm," Dani conceded, turning her attention to several suspiciously plastic sleeknesses around them.

Then she saw the Guildsman.

He *had* cammed, and there was no way of telling how long he had been watching them, leaning against the old stone wall in pebbly anonymity. Dani quietly pointed him out to Ryan.

The Guildsman straightened, and the color of his armor swam and shifted and bleached away, leaving him the color of old bronze under the mixed light. The partying Wolkenheimers flowed around him in unbroken streams, unperturbed by the predator in their midst.

After all, it was Symmetry Fair, and if someone had the morbid sense of humor to dress up as a faceless assassin, why, let him, then.

And if it wasn't a costume—well, no one in his right mind would knowingly cross a Guildsman.

Without seeming to, Den Ryan studied the street around them, considering the vulnerable, unsuspecting crowds of Fairgoers.

"We have to get him out of this crowd, first thing," he said. "If we start anything here, they'll be hauling burned bystanders out by the vanload."

"Wonderful." Dani grimaced. "How did we get into this, anyway?"

"We were here; we were convenient—"

"We were screwed."

"That, too."

"This was supposed to be a vacation."

"'Duty knows no rest.' The manual says so."

"Lucky for them we're such idealists. Dammit, Den, he's got *armor!*"

"So next year we take our vacation somewhere else. That street we just passed looked reasonably empty. Good enough?"

"Considering that he's probably heard every word we've said, it'll have to be. Let's get it done."

The Guildsman stepped away from the wall. The coded thought, drilled into him until it was virtually an autonomic response, wiped the pebbly camouflage pattern from his body. The street and its denizens, garish enough to the unaided eye, took on hallucinatory proportions for him through the optical boosting and tracking aids that picked out his quarry. A muted tingling at the backs of his wrists whispered of his plasma gauntlets' readiness. He considered how easy it would be to protect himself now with a single broad gesture that would sweep his opponents away in ashes and blue flame. But the crowds were a deterrent. Too many excess deaths and his arrangement with the Confederacy would be imperiled; they would be unwilling to associate themselves with such butchery, even to obtain what he offered them. And more, such wholesale murder would make him too much like that which he fled, would deny him the humanity he sought to reassert in the name of bloody-handed necessity.

Mutterings swelled and faded in his ears as the suit's audio system filtered crowd noises away and highlighted Dani and Ryan's conversation. He listened to them on a course of action; for a moment, the desire rose in him to spite them simply by walking in the opposite direction, leaving them to wait in their futile ambush. But then they could yet find him again, at a less opportune time, when he might not be aware of their presence until the lasers were flaring at his back. . . .

Moving smoothly, graceful in the power of his armor, he stepped into the street and started after them.

The street was empty when he turned the corner, a block-long gauntlet he was compelled to run.

The Guildsman stood unafraid in the intersection, trusting, as his hunters did, in the defenseless crowds around him to shield him from immediate attack. But he would lose that protection the instant he started down the narrow cross-street toward the next avenue and its streams of revelers.

He studied the street carefully. There were no open windows, no doors left ajar, no betraying heatshadows behind the few parked vehicles. The street itself was almost empty, with little in it to attract Fairgoers, the only traffic a few passersby venturing from one avenue to the other. Even at full magnification, the rooftops seemed untenanted; not that they could have reached them so quickly in any case. The only place where his observation failed him was at the mouth of a narrow alley, whose depths remained unfathomable from his position.

The Guildsman brought his arms up from his sides and cocked his fists downward. The tingling at his wrists increased, and the arming telltales of the gauntlets illuminated the inside of his visor. The targeting marks flashed into view, shifting with each movement of his arms as he moved toward the alleyway. He paused just at its corner, readying himself, and then blue fire lit the alley as he swung around, firing.

Aesthetic appreciation of the feminine form was all to the good, but there were other urges not so conveniently suppressed. Human beverages, while not potent enough to leave Óin more than heavily buzzed, were having another unavoidable effect.

The alley was long, it was dark, and it was convenient. Óin entered it, fumbling with a fastening seemingly designed, like all its brethren, to resist opening in direct proportion to immediacy of need.

He settled himself behind a large pile of rubbish that screened him from the street, sighed with the pleasure of overdue release—and the alley blew up. There was a flash of blue light and a crackling noise. Something fell heavily against his rubbish heap, spattering him with garbage.

He lurched into the open, fumbling with his fly, just in time to see Ryan's burning body slide off the rubbish heap to the ground. Then a tall, faceless figure appeared past the flaming corpse, standing poised with extended arm and bent wrist, fist wreathed in a cerulean halo.

It was the relative slowness of human reactions that saved him then rather than his own drunken response. He lurched forward as the Guildsman noticed him and began to turn his way. Óin slammed a three-fingered fist clumsily against the Guildsman's chest. The blow threw the assassin back against the alley wall, and he disappeared beneath a small avalanche of collapsing trash.

The garbage erupted with streamers of blue energy as the Guildsman fired blindly while he struggled to free himself. The plasma charges struck walls and junk, setting filth alight. The air thickened with the tang of ozone and the stink of burning offal. Óin wasn't drunk enough to face that. He grabbed up a trashbin and flung it roughly in the direction of the killer, then turned and bolted for the far end of the alley. He took one step and barged into something that let out an explosive *whoof!* He tried to bull past whatever it was, but it tangled in his legs as it fell and brought him down. He came to his knees and saw the girl curled up in a gasping ball, black hair fanned out on the alley floor. Behind her, the Guildsman lurched free of the encumbering junk, a great starred crack marring his left breast, shoulders hunched in anger. His fists were invisible within balls of blue radiation.

Something metallic—a silver tube with a lens at one end—glittered near the stunned girl. Óin took it up—it was something to throw if nothing else—and his over-sized grip depressed the stud on the tube.

The finger-thick scarlet thread gouged a foot-long scar in the ground before Óin realized it was a weapon and turned it on the Guildsman. The laser swept the side of the alley, cutting a wavering gash the length of the wall, coolant fumes spouting from the weapon with a whistling shriek. The beam leaped across the street as Óin swung it clear of the wall, ripping into the face of the building across from the alley. It scored the ribs of the Guildsman as he twisted desperately aside, trying to evade it. Óin swung it to follow him—and the single-pulse laser cut out with a final *crack*, leaving the burned-out tube warm in Óin's hand. The assassin had fallen and was now struggling to his knees, a faceless marionette miming pain.

Óin didn't wait to see if he made it. He grabbed the girl up under one arm and ran for the end of the alleyway, away from the flames and the Guildsman. There was a shabby fence blocking access to the street beyond. Óin went at it at a dead run and jumped.

If he'd been wholly sober, he'd have made it. If the girl hadn't been there to throw his balance off, he'd have made it. He wasn't. She was. He didn't.

His trailing foot caught the edge of the fence and slammed him down squarely atop a drink vendor's cart.

He picked his way out of the tangled wreckage, ignoring the screams of the scattered drinkers and the curses of the vendor, and moved off into the crowds. Foul smoke began to waft over the fence, adding to the confusion.

By the time the Guildsman vaulted the fence a second later, clumsy in his savaged armor, Óin and his burden were nowhere to be seen. The sprawled people around the drink cart stared at him in sudden silence, certain without reason that this was no costumed player. He stood there, faceless and grim with his wounds, turned his blank visor toward them, and raised a fist. There was a faint hum, the slightest scent of ozone, the least tinge of blue radiance.

Half a dozen prudent hands quickly pointed out Óin's path.

Wordlessly, because to speak would have been to give voice to the pain that racked his side, the Guildsman set off in pursuit. He moved slowly, giving his armor time to heal. His chest ached from Óin's fist, and he held his arm pressed tight against his side to ease the strain on the laser scar. Current flowed through the layered symbioplast as the armor drew on its enerpacs to fuse the damaged sections into a new whole.

The Guildsman was angry. He'd figured the setup and reversed the intended ambush on its planners perfectly. That should have been the end of it. And then that *creature* had reared up out of the garbage to turn a clear victory into barest survival.

Worry overshadowed anger. Óin had been a bad shock to the Guildsman, because he *was* a Guildsman, however reluctantly, and he had been counting on the skills and equipment of his position to keep him alive long enough to forswear them—and some shaggy little gnome had bounced him off a wall as if he were nothing, armor and all.

Resolution overshadowed worry. The Guildsman— how he hated that, how he hated knowing that whatever else, whatever his motives, whatever his *name*, he was a Guildsman and nothing more—had sworn that he would be free of the Guild and all its works. Any agents of the Guild, be they man, woman, or trash-spattered troll, would have to take their own chances.

The only option left to him was to turn upon his hunters. They were his equal in every element of his trade, he knew, lacking only the immediate physical advantage the armor gave him. And that fear that had driven him to cross the vast depths of interstellar space in his flight would not let him hope he could go unfound in the time left before his final disappearance.

Triply armored, then, in plastic and anger and self-pity, the Guildsman slipped through the uncaring crowds, in search.

He felt like hell.

The physical exertions and emotional stimulus of his encounter with the Guildsman had taken the shine off Óin's drunk, leaving him restless and uncomfortable and annoyed at missing both his chemical pleasures and the cathartic release of a good brawl. The clash with the assassin hadn't lasted long enough to be enjoyable. Besides, it was hardly an engagement worth boasting about, lurching around an alley throwing garbage cans with one hand and hitching at his trousers with the other.

He was moving back toward the lighter fields, responding to some half-formed urge to get back into familiar territory. On closer examination, the notion was amusing. A *gal-adheni* in the service of the Consortium was a long way from *any* familiar territory.

At least the girl over his shoulder seemed to be feeling better. She was wheezing and hawking much more comfortably as they entered the shabby little hotel on the fringe of the port district.

It was an elderly structure of weathered stone and permaplast, one of the oldest buildings in Hansen's Landing. Other buildings of its period had been carefully preserved as monuments to the colony's history. This one preserved an even older tradition, serving as a discreet bundling-house where men in from the outlying districts could partake of the port whores in safe anonymity. A man and woman—even a *gal-adheni* and a woman—entering such a place would attract no attention, and it was a quick way to get off the street.

Óin was sure the hotel would have a vacancy. If nothing else, they could always use the ex-badgerman's flat.

The cadaverous Jirin clerk looked up, and his crest sagged as he saw the blocky little alien stump into the lobby. For a moment, he feverishly considered summoning the house's complement of bouncers. Then he discarded the notion. Several of them weren't bad sorts, as bouncers went, and he didn't particularly want to see them damaged.

"Must be a new girl in the neighborhood," the clerk simpered, making a sibilant mess of the Consortium Trade Tongue. "Usually they have to carry the customers in. Oh, well, she'll learn soon enough, I'm sure."

"I'm sure," Óin agreed. "And in the meantime she'll probably give me my money's worth. Now may I have a room?"

"Oh, sir," moaned the clerk, "much as it pains me, and truly, it *does* grieve me, for I shouldn't wish you to think that we hold past differences against our customers, I'm afraid that we have no—"

Óin stabbed a thick finger down on the desk bell. There was a strangled *pingk* as the bell crumpled and the plunger was driven half its length through the base and into the surface of the desk.

"—but perhaps I can find something for you," the clerk finished. It was a quick search.

Óin took the keyplate and turned for the lift. The dilapidated tube-door slid back three inches and jammed.

"Oh, sir?" the clerk ventured. Óin turned to look at him, one hand gripping the door. A firm shove and it slid open with a rasp of stripping gears.

"Yes?" Óin extended a foot into the cylinder and stopped the rising plate. The clerk regretted having opened its mouth but pressed on with unlizardly courage.

"Sir, I am obliged to inquire as to whether the lady is accompanying you willingly . . ."

Dani wheezed.

"Satisfied?" Óin asked. The plate was making thwarted little humming noises as it tried to rise past his foot.

"Oh, yes, sir, quite satisfied, thank you."

"That's good."

The old lift plate wallowed under their combined weight. Óin tried to give it a boost with a sharp slap against the tube wall. He didn't quite manage to unbalance the plate completely.

The room was identical to the last one he'd taken there, a single room with an attached bathroom, one large bed, and a cheap set of drawers. There were no kitchen facilities; no one ever stayed in such a place long enough to cook. The permaplast walls had been left their natural dead-fishbelly shade, enhanced in places with liberal applications of dirt and smears of prestoplast sealing over the casual vandalism of previous tenants.

The bed hadn't been tuned since the day it had been installed. The girl sank nearly to the grids when Óin put her down, then bobbed back up within the frame.

Óin went into the bathroom. His tunic was a mess of soot from the alley and stains from his kamikaze dive on the drink cart. He pulled it off and rinsed it out in the dirty sink, then hung it in the shower to dry. He filled the basin and began splashing cold water on his face, trying to clear away his internal bleariness by washing off the external dirt.

Dani gathered herself, focused her will, and took a long, deep breath against the fading paralytic shrieks of her abused solar plexus. She opened her eyes, and the

56

empty, floating feeling explained itself. She was drifting in the erratic field of a decrepit bed, in a room whose tawdriness was scarcely concealed by the gaudy Fairlight flickering through the grimy window.

She lay suspended in the bed, reviewing her situation before choosing a course of action. The major elements came back readily—laying the ambush in the sidestreet; the Guildsman surprising them by bursting into the alley firing; Ryan missing his shot and dying in the mouth of the alley; a strange, squat creature erupting from the garbage and attacking the Guildsman, then slamming into her like a runaway van—

Den Ray was dead. The knowledge forced itself to the forefront of her awareness and made a mockery of her cool, professional assessments, because it was no longer a cool, professional matter to her.

The Guildsman had been a job, like many jobs she and Den Ryan had handled in the past five years. There had been no emotional involvement in it beyond the usual pride in their own ability she and Ryan had shared. There had been no love between them, no overwhelming, exclusive involvement between them. But they'd been together for five years, and she knew Den Ryan, knew how he felt and thought and acted, what he'd tell her and what he'd keep to himself. He had been a friend, in a world and a craft that put a premium on isolation. That made it hurt. That made it hurt a lot.

The memories came less clearly then, melding into a disjointed montage of smoke and sidewalks and inverted feet passing her, and then the room itself.

The sound of running water and splashing came from beyond the bathroom door. Dani rose quietly from the bed and slipped to the front door. She tried the latch.

"It's locked," declared a voice from the bathroom in oddly accented Terric.

So. The door was locked. It was doubtful she could pick the lock before whoever it was behind the voice came out. Dani was trained to assume that whoever it was would not willingly surrender the keyplate. The situation required simplification.

A figure appeared in the bathroom doorway, and Dani snapped a precise *jungeri* kick into it. It would have taken a human solidly in the chest, stealing their wind and perhaps breaking a rib or two as well.

It caught Óin Ceiragh square in the throat.

The backhanded slap, even half-checked as it was, numbed Dani's shoulder and threw her across the bed. She fell against the wall and landed sitting in the corner, the silver gun from her boot top steady in her hand.

Óin stood where she'd kicked him, rubbing his abused windpipe. He should have been dead. He wasn't. It was easy to see why.

He was built like a tree stump. His trapezius muscles were so massively developed that it seemed as if his leonine head rested directly atop his shoulders, without the complication of an intervening neck. His arms were as thick around as her thighs, the flexor groups in the forearms nearly as well developed as the biceps and triceps. His torso made not the slightest concession to a waist, flowing straight from shoulders to hips, with deep, perfect cuts that would have made a human bodybuilder forswear his calling.

He was the first *gal-adheni* she had ever seen, and he stood all of four and a half feet tall.

"You're a Dwarf," she said.

He withdrew a hand the color of tanned bark from under his thick beard and scowled at her. The lowered hand brushed the side of his knee. He had fierce black eyes.

"I've been called that," he admitted sourly. "Actually, though, I'm just about average size for my height." His voice was like heavy stones tumbling down a hillside. He glared at the small pistol in her hand.

"If you shoot me with that thing and I ever hear about it, I'll be terribly cross with you," he warned.

Dani studied him for a moment and slipped the gun back into her boot. He was probably right. He exuded the same air of scarcely tapped vitality she had seen in a Kodiak bear once on a rare visit to Terra. He could be killed readily enough, she was certain, but he wouldn't die easily. Or alone.

"I'll take your word for it," she said. "Why are you holding me here?"

"I never said I was holding you," Óin answered. "I said it was locked. You never asked for the key." He was sober now, to his annoyance. A gal-adheni had to work at a drunk; their active metabolisms broke down weak alien intoxicants too quickly.

"May I have the key?"

"You can have the whole room if you want," Óin said. "I'm leaving just as soon as my tunic dries. And I get an explanation."

"An explanation of what?"

"Of what, she asks. Of anything now, anything at all: the weather, your philosophy of life, why somebody would burn down an alley trying to kill you, anything like that. Whatever you wish."

"It's mid-Trollsday. I'm a Reform Buddhist—well, lapsed."

"That's nice, whatever it is. And—"

Dani looked up at him, sitting in her corner, hands draped across her knees. "He's a Guildsman."

"That means nothing to me."

"No, it wouldn't, would it? We don't exactly advertise the Guild to the Consortium." She shrugged. "He's an assassin."

Assassin. To a *gal-adheni*, from his world of insular clans and bloodfeuds and border contests, of honorable challenges and open confrontation, a word loaded with evil connotations.

Yet it was the first familiar thing he'd encountered since taking the Consortium Mercantile's colors. The wonder of roaming the stars, he thought bitterly.

"Why would an assassin be after you?"

"He isn't. Wasn't."

"Then why should you be troubling him?"

"It's my job."

"You serve the Confederacy, then?"

"It's the armor," she said. "The Confederacy has nothing like it. They'd do anything to get hold of a sample."

"It didn't seem so impressive to me."

"Who ran, you or him?" Dani asked. Óin grumbled something unintelligible. "Symbioplast armor is the closest thing to a perfect individual combat system in the Confederacy. It's tough as hell—but I see you discovered that," she finished, eying his bloody knuckles.

"I put a fair dent in him."

Dani looked at him with renewed interest. "If that's true, it's impressive. Guild armor will turn anything short of a two-by-fifty sliver or a heavy battle laser."

"Do you have those?"

"I had a laser."

"The tube thing? I used that. It didn't work."

"Then I've got a problem."

"If you go after him again, you do. I wouldn't. I'd just as soon not even see him again."

"Well, I have to."

"Why?"

"It's my job."

"Creac's eyes, a patriot. I haven't seen many of those out here."

"It's an old-fashioned virtue, true." She smiled. "Besides, I'm no patriot, just a professional, I'd like to think."

"Well, there's little enough of either quality around to see it go to waste like that. You don't have another laser?"

"How many do you think we carry? I've got a gun, but it's only a two by ten, some sun pellets, and a knife. I've still got my breaking and entering kit, but I really don't think he'll stand still long enough to let me pick the seals on his armor."

"What about your friend? Was he carrying anything else?"

"Well if he was, it won't do me a whole hell of a lot of good now, will it?" she asked, the bitterness welling up in spite of herself. "It burned with him."

"Yes. . . ." Óin said, unsettled by her show of emotion. He made a vague gesture with one hand, wanting to touch her, console her, but she was too far from where he stood. The act would have been too awkward, exaggerated, false. He let the hand drop.

"I'm sorry about that," he said lamely.

"You can spare me that," she snapped. "You never even met him. It isn't any loss to you."

"No, I suppose it isn't," Óin agreed, embarrassed.

Dani shook her head disgustedly and noticed the smears and stains defacing her own clothing. "Shit. I can't go out there like this. Excuse me." She brushed past Óin into the bathroom. Óin stood waiting while water ran and splashed.

Dani came back into the room, wringing out her sodden tunic. Óin couldn't picture anything so small confronting the terror of that alley. It seemed an insuperable burden to place on so slender a back.

"Look, then, if your Confederacy wants this so badly, why don't you call in more help? Why try and finish this thing alone?"

"Because it's my job. And he owes me now."

"So he does. But I don't think it's a debt you can collect on your own."

"There isn't much of any other way I'm going to do it."

"I think there is."

Dani looked at him. "By god, I think the man— excuse the term—is volunteering. Why? Sympathy for the poor Earthgirl's dire plight?"

"Maybe I just like vengeful patriots." Óin grinned. "In any case, I certainly didn't say anything about volunteering. I'm a loyal servant of the Consortium, *aya*—?"

"Yuen. Dani Yuen."

"*Aya* Yuen. And as a loyal servant of the Consortium, I should certainly expect some compensation for my services."

"Such as?"

"Buy out the remainder of my contract. I'll get your assassin for you. You just send me home once I do."

"What's the balance of your contract?"

"Six years' service at twelve thousand Consortium Credit Units a year."

"You're joking."

"A servant of the Consortium? About business? Never, *aya*."

"No, that would be out of character, wouldn't it. But seventy-two thousand CCUs for one job?"

"Among other coin. But consider this before you answer—I put a dent in him once before, when I was falling down drunk with my pants around my knees. I can do better this time, I'm sure. And if I can, can you afford not to hire me?"

"No. I don't suppose I can."

"This is getting very sloppy."

The Guildsman was impresed. The man who had identified himself as a Confederate agent was dressed as garishly as any farmer in from the field for Symmetry Fair, and yet he managed to remain as faceless as the Guildsman himself. He adjusted the bright, cheap scarf around his throat with a hand whose enlarged foreknuckles clashed with an impeccable manicure. Someone who took such care of his fingers probably shouldn't spend so much time punching *makiwara* posts, the Guildsman thought. "We have accorded you a considerable degree of leeway in your conduct of this affair, simply and entirely because of the opportunity you present us. But you must realize that *I* at least have superiors, and *they* are beginning to wonder if perhaps we shouldn't demand a stronger input into the resolution of this matter."

"No," the Guildsman said, his voice flat and filtered through the armor's speakers. "No. We will do this my way or not at all. You want the armor, and I will give it to you. I wish to escape the Guild, and you will give me the means to do that. But you will not control that means."

The agent made the same precise, pointless adjustment to his scarf once again. "But we have resources of our own, you know. We could make this much easier for you. We could provide an identity, a completely developed history—"

"No. You underestimate the influence of the Guild. You do not realize how pervasive their networks are. I want absolutely no contact with you that I cannot avoid. All I need from you is an authorization to board any Confederate Fleet Arm ship of my choice. No names, no notifications, no records, and the authority to send it to any port in the Confederacy I choose. I wish simply to drop out of the system entirely and to choose my own course of action from there. That way, I have a chance to live. No other."

"That's difficult to arrange. It requires action by an extremely high authority, and such people are not inclined to act on the urgings of a professional killer, particularly from the opposition."

"They'll do it." The Guildsman thumped a fist against his armored breast. "For this. They want it badly enough."

The hand rose, to fondle bright fabric again. "Yes. Most probably. And that brings us to our second point."

"What second point?"

"What my superiors want. You are quite correct. The armor is our first desire. But the situation has changed. You are no longer the only Guildsman we are aware of in Hansen's Landing. There are at least two others: those who hunt you."

"One other. They found me already."

"I see. In any case, my superiors feel that a Guildsman's armor *and* a Guildsman to interrogate about it would be of even greater value than the armor alone—"

"Forget it. I've had enough of being used by the Guild; why should I consent to being used by you?"

"Because you must contend with them, anyway."

"For myself. You aren't listening. I've killed for the Guild, killed the people they told me to kill, for no better reason than it served their purposes. Now you want me to kill or capture these two—I'm not anticipating you, am I? Good—because it will serve your purposes. But I will not serve anybody's purposes anymore, do you understand? Living is my purpose now, and nothing else."

"Do you think you can convince them of that?"

"I'm not interested in convincing them of that. I just want to get away from them."

"They've found you once."

"And I killed one of them. If they find me again, I may kill the rest of them. But if I have to, it will be for myself. Not for your superiors. Is that clear?"

"I will make your views known. When shall we meet again?"

"When you have my authorizations."

"We should like to keep in closer touch. This situation is becoming disquieting."

"And I do not wish to expose myself to your organization. I will not take unnecessary risk. This contact is an unnecessary risk."

The hand stopped halfway to the scarf, balling into a fist.

"What?"

"I'm sure your superiors have heard every word we've spoken here. You might be an unnecessary risk."

"I might. But you need me, or you have no contact with us."

"I don't believe you're not being monitored."

"Believe it. Check."

The Guildsman directed his suit sensors outward. The agent was bare of any telltales that might have indicated a body wire. The shadowed plaza offered up no distant surveillants.

The agent smiled tightly. "I thought it might be necessary to *make* myself necessary, you see. If you want my superiors to hear your demands, I'll have to live to repeat them." He gave his scarf a final fussy tug. "And you can be sure your authorizations will be delivered via dead-letter-drop." He backed off into the dark, and he was gone, leaving the Guildsman alone in the plaza with his resolve and the realization that his only real safety lay in the deaths of his hunters.

The only way to find the Guildsman was to go out into the streets and let him try to kill them.

Óin and Dani moved through the Fair-crowded streets. They looked at the windows, and they looked at the doors. They looked at the crowds around them, but the Guildsman was not to be found, not in such a press.

Brazen Trollshulm had set, leaving the streets lit only by the pacific green glow of Hansenwald and the wild Fair lighting.

"I can't grasp this," Óin said. "How could an entire *guild* of assassins exist? Why isn't it put down?"

"The armor, for one thing," Dani said. "What do you put something like that down with?"

"With numbers, if nothing else. There can't be so many of them that they can dominate an opposed populace, can there?"

"Maybe not. But who says the populace opposes them?"

"What?"

"Why should the populace oppose the Guild?"

"Why should—they're *assassins*, *aya*! It's your own name for them."

"Mm-hmm. So?"

"So?" Óin was beyond further comment.

Dani looked at him with a mixture of worldly amusement and curiosity. "What's so astonishing? You said *adhe* knows assassins; you must know what they are."

65

"Of course we know what they are! That's why we despise them!"

"Is it? What do your assassins do?"

Óin gaped at her. He would have had a readier answer had she asked him what a tree did, or a rock. "What does any assassin do? He's a murderer, a treacherous killer of heroes too bold to be slain in honest challenge, of leaders whose *sgeadhanha-dan* is too vigorous to oppose. That's what an assassin does."

"Oh." They walked on several spaces. "It's not their name for themselves, you know."

"What?"

"The Guild. They don't call themselves assassins, actually."

"Don't they? Then what do they call themselves?"

"The Guild of Resolution."

"What?"

"The Guild of Resolution. The Guild considers itself a political instrument of last resort. What do you know of Earth?"

"Little enough. More than I care to if they don't know how to call an assassin an assassin."

"There are twelve billion people on Earth. That may be too many. It certainly doesn't leave much room for making mistakes. Correcting them could be expensive—in resources, in lives. And how do you decide whether or not it *is* a mistake? Who makes the judgment? Who with the power to make the judgment is competent to make the judgment?"

"Is that their justification? The people are too spineless to right their own wrongs, so they go and hire murderers?"

"No one hires a Guildsman. The Guild picks its own victims by its own rules. If the Terran Council is being pressured to loosen the birth laws, then the Guild kills a few of the louder bishops or maharishis. If some industrial magnate insists on plowing under the last of the rain forests in spite of the oxygen generation loss, the

66

Guild just kills him rather than let him get away with it through all the years of legal bickering that would otherwise follow."

"Are you defending them, then?"

Dani sighed. "They're gun law. Their example encourages fanatics to emulate them, although the Guild has the decency to eliminate the more rabid amateurs themselves. But they serve a purpose, you can't get around that. I suppose the best thing you can say about the Guild is that things might be worse without it."

"If you feel that way, then why are you willing to go against them?"

Dani's mouth hardened. "I've got a job to do."

"That, and they killed a friend?"

"I've got a job to do."

Óin chuckled. "'Eochain Long-Hair'."

"What?"

"'Eochain Long-Hair.' An old *gal-adheni* song. Eochain Long-Hair was the daughter of a *baredan*, a clan-lord, whose *sgeadhanha-dan* was befouled by ambition and whose kin rose and slew him. She was sympathetic to the rebels, but she knew her duty to her father and sought out the rebel leaders in turn and slew them. It's a very long song about honor and dignity and the virtues of maidens."

Dani smiled. "Well, that lets me out, that last bit."

"There are virtues other than chastity," Óin said. "That's what the song was about."

"Oh."

The crowd scattered before the armored man like gaily colored tropical fish before some great predator of the reefs.

A groundvan, rash enough to risk the Fair-jammed streets, jolted to a sudden halt as the white-clad figure suddenly appeared before it.

The harassed driver, brave in his ignorance, leaned out of his cab and hurled a stream of profanity at the Guildsman's receding back.

The Guildsman ignored the curses, just as he ignored the protests and glares of the people he shoved roughly from his path in his effort to keep sight of the couple ahead of him.

The Guildsman had found his prey.

The lighter field stretched out before them, empty at this odd hour save for the hulking shapes of several ships and service gear, the perfect place for some discreet violence.

"I think it's time we discussed that other coin you mentioned," Dani said.

"Do you? And why now, of a sudden?"

"Because your job was about a hundred meters behind us at that last intersection."

"Ah, indeed." The fence bordering the lighter field was nothing formidable—after all, making smuggling too difficult would have been bad for business. The lock on the service gate crumpled like foil in Óin's hand.

Óin and Dani walked out onto the flat permaplast apron of the field. Behind them, past the city, the sun was rising. A roseate glow began to stain the sky above the garish buildings, driving back the false green "daylight."

Ahead of them, the swollen bulk of an intrasystem freighter loomed up out of its launch pit. In the glare of the field lights on their graceful pylons, they could see that at least one naval architect in the Confederacy had a sense of humor: emblazoned around the top of the grossly distended cargo section was the name *Gravid*.

"Can he see us now, do you think?" Óin asked.

"No, I think he'll have to come out onto the field after us. But he'll pick up our heat shadow before he sees us properly."

"Good. Now, what's the question about my payment? As I said before, you need my services; you can't afford not to hire me."

"I know that. But I'm limited as to what I can offer

you personally, and those seventy-two thousand CCUs are going to cause enough trouble. I wouldn't want you to think you were being taken advantage of or anything." She finished a little archly, watching the way they'd come. The field stayed empty.

"Well, now, that's a noble sentiment, and I appreciate the thought; yes I do. Of course, I'd have appreciated it even more if you'd brought this up before I was stuck between your assassin out there and an empty field."

"You can call this off any time you like."

"I know that, but I'd still have to get past him to do so, wouldn't I?"

Dani grinned. "So I practiced a little enlightened self-interest."

Óin chuckled. Service with the Basiri had at least given him an appreciation for sharp dealing. "In any case, I've already been paid in the coin in question, thank you."

Dani's grin faded. "You have? How?"

"Takes a bit of explaining. . . ."

"Am I going somewhere?"

"Well, simply put, I've been three years in the service of the Consortium, and do you know, this is the first time in three years I've had the slightest idea what I was doing. I've seen six worlds and liked none of them, fought a war and never knew why. But I did it because it was the only way I could ever afford to start a holding of my own, back home, and that was the one thing I wanted more than anything. And now you come along with this assassin of yours, and that's good. For I know what an assassin is, even if you try to tell me differently, and I know what to do about them and why. That's a feeling I haven't had in a long time. So my extra payment is taken care of nicely, I should think. Thank you."

There was a silence. Dani had no response that she could give him.

There was a flicker of movement at the service gate

they'd entered by—not much, just the least glimpse of something moving.

It was enough.

Óin Ceiragh turned and looked at Dani Yuen, grinning broadly as he contemplated killing one of the two human beings on Wolkenheim he thought he understood.

"Let's get it done," he said.

The Guildsman began to pick up speed as he moved through the concealing equipment. The lambent, crackling auras that encased his fists barely matched the hot flame in the pit of his stomach. The energy coursing through his plastic skin made a barely fit companion for the driving excitement building in his chest. It was over. He would finish it now, here, and it would be over. Then he would meet the Confederate agent, hand over the armor, and be a free man, a new man.

The machinery rested black on the permaplast around him, cooler than the dawn breeze that passed over it. Ahead and just to his left there was a faint infrared shadow outlining a small cart unit right up against a lighter's hull. His sensors, attuned to his quarry's distinctive trace, had marked the glow with luminous green telltales.

A figure—the troll!—broke from the machine's concealment. The Guildsman swung, raising his fist—and Óin was gone from sight behind another machine. Arm extended, the Guildsman stalked forward, moving with predatory, confident grace, keeping half an eye on Óin's original hiding place.

There was a sudden knowledge of movement as a tiny something struck the pavement before him. There was nothing to be seen but *light* and then *black* as the sun pellet detonated. The armor's optics tried frantically to cope with the sudden brilliance, dropped shields— and blinded the Guildsman.

The Guildsman went with his first, animal response,

lashing out with blue fire at Óin's new hiding place. But Óin was already moving, head averted to spare his sight. He braced his legs against a heavy generator cart and pushed off with a force that set the cart skidding several feet. Óin rocketed into the Guildsman's back, making the assassin cry out, a horrible, scratching sound through the armor's distorting filters. Only the armor saved the Guildsman's spine.

The *gal-adheni* straightened as the Guildsman stumbled forward. The killer was turning even as he lurched upright, desperately quick for a human, but a measured and stately pace next to high-gravity-quickened *gal-adheni* reflexes. Óin slipped a hand under the slowly rising arm and flipped it up above the Guildsman's head, then drove two quick punches into the assassin's chest.

The symbioplast didn't quite yield before the first blow; it landed atop the thickened repair where Óin's alley punch had landed. The second struck the sternum, and fresh cracks marred the plastic's surface.

It wasn't a fight. The Guild armor was incredibly powerful, perhaps even stronger than Óin's natural strength. But the man within was a human man, with human responses, and against the frighteningly fast Óin Ceiragh, he was completely ineffective.

To Dani, it was like watching a demonstration back in training, like watching the wizened Okinawan who had taught them unarmed combat humiliate a brawny trainee cocksure and overreliant on his own strength. Óin would slap one or the other of the lethal plasma gauntlets up out of line and plunge in with a punishing attack to the Guildsman's body before he could react. When the assassin's counter finally came, he would be somewhere else, behind him or to the other side, ready to start again. The armor was absorbing most of the punishment, as it had been designed to do, but the blows were beginning to work their way in to the soft flesh and bone underneath.

It was chance that felled Óin Ceiragh.

He weaved around and behind the Guildsman, under his useless, upraised arm, and jabbed an elbow back into the armored man's kidney. The assassin spasmed, reflexively yanking his arm down—and his armored elbow drove with its full force into Óin's shoulder. Óin bellowed in astonishment and pain as the joint separated, and the Guildsman, following through on the initial contact, brought his forearm down on the back of Óin's neck.

Óin straightened up through the scarlet fog that enveloped him and brought his good fist around in a backhanded punch that crushed the seals of the Guildsman's visor and stripped it away. But the twisting pressure of his dangling arm on his ruined shoulder thickened the redness around him again, and when it cleared, he was looking at the Guildsman's fist, surrounded with blue energy. The Guildsman's eyes locked with his, wide with pain and shockingly blue. There was a deep gash on one cheek where the ruined visor had gouged his face. Óin felt the touch of the plasma gauntlet's conductance beam—

The assassin's face dissolved in a scarlet froth as Dani fired a half-second burst of slivers into it. The arm dropped limply away as the assassin, ruined head cradled in the remaining fragment of helmet, fell back and lay still.

There was a moment's peace, an instant's stasis on the lighter field. The sky overhead was largely blue now as Hansen's Primary itself rose above the buildings. Only along the far horizon did a slight aquamarine tinge mark Hansenwald's setting. In the distance, the Fairlights were beginning to flicker off, their fascination lost in the mundane daylight.

The ruined armor registered the death within it, and the destruct circuit faithfully triggered its overload on the enerpacs. Óin lurched backward, clutching at his injured arm, as the Guildsman was reduced to slag and ash in a final burst of energy.

Óin staggered back from the heat and sat down, heavily, against a cart. Dani came up, slipping her pistol back into her boot.

"*Ai, shta*," Óin cursed mechanically. "*Shta. Ai, Shta.*" He looked up, frustration and pain etched across his face. "I'm sorry," he said. "I'm sorry. I didn't know that would happen. I didn't. . . ."

Dani didn't look at him. Instead, she kept her eyes on the puddle of ruined plastic at her feet.

"I did," she said quietly.

"What?"

"You did fine," Dani assured him. "Just fine."

"But the armor's ruined! It's worthless now."

Dani finally looked at him. "That was the idea."

Óin floundered, groggy with pain and confusion, groping for understanding.

"It's like I said before," Dani explained. "The armor is the only thing that keeps the Guild going. We couldn't let the Confederacy get hold of a sample."

Óin stared at her, sick with sudden knowledge.

Dani frowned at his expression. "I told you I was no patriot," she said, as though answering a spoken accusation. "Just a professional. Although maybe I am at that. I don't know. I don't pretend to be an expert on these things. I just do what seems right."

She looked around. In the distance, they could see the flashing lights of a field security groundvan.

"I can't stay here," she said. "The police will get your arm taken care of. Don't worry about any trouble. You just killed a Guildsman, remember? You'll be a hero to them. We'll contact the Consortium about your contract."

He didn't answer. He just stared at her and felt the corruption welling within him.

Dani's frown wavered, and when she spoke again, there was no mockery in her voice.

"You shouldn't put your faith in the virtues of maidens," she said, and walked away out of sight among the machines.

Óin exhaled, a slow, shuddering sob. He looked up. The sun was well above the skyline now, the streets deserted as the Fair crowds retired to await the next rising of the binaries. The Fair decorations looked grotesque, tawdry and out of place in the strong daylight, like most illusions.

Chapter Four

"That's it, then?" Cian asked the grizzled *aidjiin*. "That's your story?"

"As best I can tell it," said Óin.

Cian set down his bowl, the food cold and untasted since Óin had begun to speak. "And does it frighten off many of your guests?"

"Some."

"But not all," said Cian. "Not even most, does it?"

"No."

"I'm not surprised," said Cian Canbhei.

"Aren't you, child?"

"How do you expect to blacken the name of the Consortium with a story of your own sorry failure? You are *aidjiin*, not them."

"I don't need you to tell me what I am," Óin said bitterly. Cian ignored him, taking down his cloak and giving it a single, ineffective twist before slinging it, still sodden, across his shoulders. "I only told you how it happened."

"Yes, how it happened," Cian turned to face him. "You forswore a proper master, a lawful master, to take an assassin's pay, out of your own weakness. That's how it happened."

"That's right, you arrogant, cane-cutting child! That's exactly how. I forswore a 'proper master, a lawful master,' who was perfectly happy to see me leave for a few coins in their own pockets. I took an assassin's pay, to kill an assassin, because I wanted to go home, to leave a world where such things were possible; *that* was my weakness!"

"That was not your concern," Cian said. "Their honor was not your concern—"

"Yes, my honor is my own concern," Óin said, "and my own failure. But is it my failure that I could not believe that Consortium and Confederation alike could shape a world where honor is so meaningless that even assassins might claim it? Was I wrong not to believe that whole peoples could be so bereft of the knowledge of simple right and wrong that I could not tell the virtuous from the villainous?"

"They are not *gal-adheni*," said Cian Canbhei. "They are not bound to accommodate themselves to your ethics."

"Then what is the point of having such wretched things at all? Creac's *balls*, child!" Óin raged. "Say something to me I haven't said to myself every hour of every day since I took the Guild's service! There must be something an honest, honorable *gal-adheni* can tell me that a verminous *aidjiin* cannot!"

"No," said Cian Canbhei. "You are *aidjiin*. There is nothing I can say to you and nothing I should. Now let me leave." He started for the door, but Óin barred his way, the point of his quarrel inches from Cian's chest.

"No," Óin said. "I may not be a proper, respectable *gal-adheni*. But how long do you think you'll last out in the Consortium if you turn and run every time you find something is not to your liking?"

The Consortium-built floater drifted silently to ground at the base of Óin's hill. The dim yellow hearth-glow shining out of the crudely shuttered windows flickered and was obscured by the driving rains and blowing *aceail* leaves.

Dani stepped down from the floater and watched its canopy seal up as though no portal had ever been there.

She pulled the hood of her robe forward and turned her back on the driving rain, staring up at the rough stone hut. It was a shabby, unimpressive sight, she thought, a perfect place for the resolution of an affair that had brought her beyond the farthest limits of her deepest faith, into the empty, frightened obedience to dogma that was all Óin Ceiragh had left to her.

She knelt before the small hold-all at her feet, opening it to reveal the plastic white sleekness of its contents. The flexible mesh of the Consortium robe clung tightly to her flesh when she pressed it down, fitting easily beneath the breastplate and gauntlets and faceless helmet.

Cian ignored the crossbow aimed at his heart, but he backed into the center of the hut.

"Canbhei don't run," he said. "I do not expect everything I find in the Consortium to be everything I think it will be. But I do expect to be able to confront it honorably. The Consortium may not be properly *gal-adheni*, *aidjiin*. But that does not mean I cannot be."

"No," Óin said. "It does not. But do you know what that may cost you?"

"I know what the Consortium wants of me. They want a *gal-adheni's* strength, a *gal-adheni's* loyalty. And I know what I want of them—I want the anonymity of Consortium service, and the chance to earn my name without putting the *sgeadhanha-dan* of my line at risk. I can give them my service for that."

Óin shook his head. "That's what you're prepared to pay. You don't know what it will cost you."

"How *can* I know?"

"Look at me. And by Creac's heart, *listen*."

Part Two

THE ROAD
ONCE TRAVELED

Chapter Five

Óin Ceiragh preferred the darkness of bars. It was the only place in his universe where he could pretend he was safe, where he could hide, for a time, from the shame he had brought upon himself.

This bar served Turnaround, the vast terminal some thirty-six thousand kilometers above the face of the Earth, that linked Terran North America with the stars. The bar looked out on the curving black edge of nightside Earth, separated from the blackness of space by a fine double line of rose and blue white where sunrise blossomed along the horizon. There had been an attempt, in the bar's early days, to design its layout with the great viewport as its floor. The attempt had been abandoned quickly. Drunken groundsiders had proven hysterically incapable of looking down and finding themselves suspended above thousands of kilometers of nothingness.

Such a simple disorientation would not have bothered Óin Ceiragh. He was unimaginably far from home, with no way back save by the grace of others, separated from his world and his clan and any possible place for himself as much by the enormity of his crime as by any physical distance, however vast.

And he was trapped. Trapped by the criminal status of the power to which his Basiri masters had sold his service at his own mistaken request. Trapped by his own sense of honor, however tarnished, which would not let him violate a commitment he had entered into willingly.

So he stood at a bar thirty-six thousand kilometers above the Earth, paying for his many drinks with the coin of the Terran Guild of Resolution. He was the youngest son of Cadhli of the line of Cumil *aereach*, Cumil the Hero, and he was the first in all the long songs of his name to kill in secret, without honor and without grievance, for simple gain.

He would have welcomed the absence of a floor. Lacking that, he merely wanted to hit something.

Dani found him easily. It was impossible to miss a *gal-adheni* Dwarf in any gathering of humans.

The bartender did not object to the space Óin took up. If he crowded out two men, he drank enough for three.

Óin couldn't avoid drawing attention; he was probably the first of his race ever to venture so near Terra. But the sullen set of his shoulders and glowering black eyes discouraged their casual curiosity.

Dani drew no notice as she moved toward the crowded bar.

Walking through the press, she held her shoulders forward and drawn slightly in, not enough to be obvious but sufficiently so as to make her look just the least bit stooped and flat-chested. She brought her hair forward over her shoulders so that it obscured her face from the sides. Shrouded in her façade of assumed plainness, she passed unnoticed up to the bar.

She moved into the empty space beside Óin, and her adopted anonymity dropped away like silk parting on a stiletto's edge.

"What the hell are you doing here?" she demanded in an angry whisper.

Óin turned toward her, slowly, deliberately.

"I," he said calmly, "am drinking. But it isn't working. I still remember you." His voice had the basso timber of some vast, distant earth movement, slow and mournful as waves breaking on some deserted coast.

"What are you doing off the ship?"

"What was I doing on the ship? Being a fool."

"Well, you're getting better at it all the time. Now let's get out of here."

"And if I shouldn't wish to?" Óin asked quietly.

"What?"

"I said, 'And if I shouldn't wish to?'" He turned to face Dani then. For the first time in long months, she caught a glimpse of the fell, ursine vitality that had so impressed her on their initial meeting in the distant Hansen system. But this time it was directed at her—and Dani suddenly realized what a daunting quality it could be. "What if I would rather shout out that here I stand, a servant of the Guild of Resolution, with one of my masters?"

"You'd die," she said, just as quietly.

"I might," Óin answered. He grinned. "But do you think I fear that? It's living that terrifies me now."

Impasse. There was no doubt that Óin was capable of exposing them both if he took it into his head that it was something his unyielding alien sense of honor demanded. Then she would have to kill him, or try—but even if she succeeded, the attempt would doom her. There was nowhere to run within the cramped confines of Turnaround.

But she knew Óin could be stopped short of that. That same sense of honor, product of the codes and customs that had shaped him, was the perfect tool for controlling him. If she was cold enough to exploit it.

"You won't do it," she said flatly, almost as a challenge.

Óin glared at her. "You think I won't?"

"I know you won't. It would be a breach of service."

Óin Ceiragh looked at her a moment longer. Then the anger drained from his expression, like water from a pierced vessel. He set his glass down among the many already on the bar and walked out without looking back, ignoring the protests of the bartender.

"Hey! Where the hell do you think you're going!? You gotta pay for the drink!"

"I'll take care of it," Dani said quickly, to forestall a call to port security. She offered the bartender her own transient's card. The man accepted it, grumbling.

"Who the hell does he think he is, anyway? Gahdam eety, he ain't nobody special."

"I think he's aware of that," Dani said.

She found him right outside the bar, among the diminutive shapes of one of the terminal's gardens. The tailored miniform trees and shrubs were larger and less subtly shaped than true bonsai. But then they had never been meant to serve as art. They had simply been twisted and distorted into a form that fit the purpose of their human shapers, providing patches of green life within Turnaround's walls of plastic and alloy. Óin looked as though he belonged there, squatting on his heels and blackly contemplating the miniform oak before him.

In some unanticipated spark of insight, the two forms suddenly seemed to blend before Dani's eyes, the oak acquiring some part of Óin's bleak and defeated mien as he took on a portion of its stunted, manipulated aspect.

The plain, vivid clarity of the impression startled her. Dani Yuen was a Guildswoman, an assassin. Pragmatism was a vital tool in that role, the sort of pragmatism that let her make the cold-equation decisions a killer had to make. Decisions like the one to use Óin Ceiragh to murder a defecting Guildsman on Wolkenheim. But illusion was a dangerous luxury, when her success and even her life could depend on an uncluttered perception of the world around her as it truly was. Metaphor was no part of her philosophy.

Yet the impression persisted.

He looked up as she approached him, silent for a space.

"You understand me too well," he said at last.

"It didn't take any great understanding to know you were afraid to die," she answered. The shadow of a twisted oak darkened in her memory.

"Ah." Óin looked back to the tree. Dani studied his expression. There was a new shading there, a new layer of disappointment. But with what? With her?

"You're wrong, you know," he said. "The dead don't fear dying."

"You aren't dead," she said a little angrily, resenting the exaggerations of an alien perspective.

Óin shook his head. "I've been dead since I killed that Guildsman on Wolkenheim," he said. "In any way that matters."

"What way is that? You made a bargain with us; you'd kill a Guildsman in return for passage back to Galatia. You carried out your end of the agreement. We'll carry out ours, and that's the end of it." Óin gave no sign that he had heard. Dani moved in front of him. She had to kneel to look him in the eye, facing him over the tiny oak. "Now you just tell me what the hell difference there is between that and playing mercenary for the Basiri."

He looked up. "The difference is, I was not an assassin."

"You were a killer. You took military service with a City Mercantile. You've told me you saw combat there. Are you going to tell me now that you never killed anybody?"

"Of course I killed. I was a warrior." He spoke the word with a pride that rang strangely on Dani's civilized ears. But then, from what she knew of it, *adhe* was not a civilized world by her standards. A culture that had not risen above the level of feuding blood clans would value its fighters. They performed a necessary public service and deserved to be honored for it. But such a culture despised its assassins.

Dani Yuen, on the other hand, was civilized. She could conceive of the result that must follow if a civilization with the power to bridge the distances

85

between the stars ever turned that energy to open warfare. She had the breeding and the conditioning to look at the choice between killing one man and reducing a world to radioactive memories and choose to kill the man. But Óin Ceiragh lacked the blessing of her worldliness. He came from a society that abhorred assassination—and he was an assassin.

"Assassin, warrior, you were a killer," she said. "You killed, and for someone else. That's all you ever did, for me, for the Basiri, for the Guild."

"But it was not right that I should do it for you."

"Why not?"

"Because the battles I fought for the Basiri were proper battles, open and just. The worlds I fought on had violated agreements with the Basiri, broken trust, and sought to do violence against them. Because the Basiri openly declared their grievances against those worlds. And because my people hold it correct to offer service to the Basiri."

"And not to assassins."

"And not to assassins." Óin nodded bleakly.

"Dammit, you didn't know I was a Guildswoman—"

"That doesn't matter."

"—and there's no reason anybody on *adhe* ever has to know, either," Dani said. "All they ever have to know when you go home is that you finished your agreed service and earned your money. You made a mistake— fine. There's no reason to advertise the fact."

Óin shook his massive head. "They would know."

"Not if you didn't tell them."

"They would know."

"How?"

Óin muttered something she couldn't make out.

"What?"

"*Tosceama shtane taya nanam*," he repeated. "'I see a thing you cannot.' We have a practice on my world, a science, a skill, an art—oh, this Terric of yours has words for so many amazing things, but it has no word for this— our word for it is *sgeadhanha-dan*. It means—the most

86

truly I know how to say it in your words is 'to see what is,' but that isn't it, not fully. . . ."

"You're talking about your world-view," Dani said. "There's a word for it in one of the old Earth languages, but I wouldn't dare try to pronounce it. You're talking about your perception of reality, of the way you believe the world to be—"

"No. It's more than that. It's not just to believe that the world is the way it is but to *know* it is so and to have it so *because* you know . . ." He shook his head. "I just don't have the words for it. I don't think your tongue has them, not the right ones. But *sgeadhanha-dan* is what is because you know it is. . . ."

Dani looked at him doubtfully. "Solipsism?"

"I don't think that is the word, because of the way you say it. *Sgeadhanha-dan* is a real thing. I never had any great skill at it—that is why I could be wrong about you—but there are those that do. I'm an assassin. It's what I know myself to be; it's what I am. Should I return to my world, even if I declared myself falsely, others would know me for what I was and reject me."

"Then where will you go?"

"Home," Óin said.

"But why—?"

"At least there *I* will know what I am. Not like here, where assassins count themselves honorable folk and an offer of lawful service brings disgrace. The knowing of such a world is beyond me; I can probably appreciate the *sgeadhanha-dan* of this sorry little tree more truly than your own," he said.

"The two of you have a lot in common," Dani said, and instantly regretted it.

Óin looked up at her, almost eagerly. "Why do you say that?"

Dani cursed silently. She could refuse to answer—

"I saw it." The topmost branches of the miniform oak underlined her view of him.

"You have experienced my *sgeadhanha-dan*," Óin said, brightening. "I told you I have little skill in the art;

I must have—expressed it, unknowing, from unadmitted need. That would be frowned on, at home. It is held to be discourteous in the extreme. I must apologize." But he did not sound repentant.

"I took no offense," Dani said.

"Ah." It was the right answer, the answer he had wanted and could have expected on *adhe*. Dani did not begrudge it; it was a small enough demand upon an assassin's compassion.

"But I still don't understand you," she said.

"That's all right," Óin said. The bleakness was leaving him, as much as it ever did. That·part of his despair that ever showed in his face was born of the drink. But with his fierce Galatian vigor, sobriety began to return almost as the glass left his hand and the darkness would retreat again, to be masked over and penned within as his own affair.

"I think you understand me as well as you need to," he said.

"Let's get back to the ship," Dani suggested.

Óin stood. "How much longer must we remain here?"

"Until the Guild can make safe arrangements for you. You present something of a novel problem for them; we've never used outsiders before."

"We have an agreement," Óin said.

"They know what they promised."

The derelict lay dead at the base of the spaceship, in sight of the stars.

The spinning lights of the port emergency services floater picked the little groups of men out of the night, engraving them in flickering bas-reliefs against the darkness. The derelict sprawled lifeless against the ship's undercarriage. The small knot of port police, sweat soaking through the backs and armpits of their white tunics in the sweltering Brazilian night air, looking off toward the approaching city ambulance. Lucaz Santiago stood looking down at the body, the floater's lights sparking briefly in his deep-set, dark eyes and painting dark shadows on the wrinkled skin, stretched tight over high cheekbones.

There was no one in there anymore, Lucaz thought as he stared at the corpse. The seams in the dead man's face, the textures of the grimy, calloused hands, were mere patterns now, like the grain of tree bark or heat cracks in pavement. They told Lucaz nothing of the character that might have animated them or the experiences that had etched them there in that inert flesh. Character had fled with life; those experiences were equally lost. Who would notice or remember the life of such a man but the one who had lived it?

The derelict's features were slack, impassive in death. Lucaz might have called them peaceful if he had wanted to lie to himself, if he had wished to minimize the finality of the derelict's death with some fancied construct of a gentle release, a surrender. He did not. Something had driven that man into the spaceport grounds, something had drawn him to the clustered ships, to die amid the great machines waiting to challenge the sky. Lucaz would not insult him by thinking he had surrendered.

The city medics were bagging the corpse now, working the body into its neat, manageable plastic shroud. One of the port cops saw Lucaz and wandered over. A sergeant, by the three gold pips on the pocket flap.

"No identification, naturally," the policeman said. He was facing the body and the working medics, but his eyes were on Lucaz. Santiago felt a moment's weariness at the start of a familiar game.

"Do they have any idea how he died, sergeant?" he asked.

The sergeant shrugged. "With such a one, who can say? The streets, maybe they killed him. Maybe the North killed him. Maybe they starved him as they starve all of us." A definite pot bulged the front of the sergeant's tunic, made of good northern synthetic.

89

Lucaz felt a moment's irritation. The policeman was talking for him, not to him, hoping the famous journalist would be inspired to work his patrol-car philosophy into his next feature.

"Maybe it's as simple as that," Lucaz agreed. But he didn't think so. He had never written about it as though it was. No quotes for you, my friend, not tonight. "How old do you think he was?"

The cop shrugged. "He is dead. And that's no age at all."

"That, at least, is true, sergeant." Lucaz moved away from the policeman, approaching the young doctor cross-signing reports with a bored corporal.

"How did he die?" Lucaz asked.

"How do they ever die?" the doctor asked. He wore the black patch of the coroner's office. He reached into the ambulance and pulled out the empty bottle, neatly wrapped and tagged and preserved for the investigation that would never be made. Certainly this young doctor would never see the results of his night's work, Lucaz knew. He was just one of the armies of indifferent subordinates who could expect nothing more from their lives than to work the night shifts and routine assignments for superiors who had risen above such mundane duties. But he was all the notice the derelict would ever get, and his signature would put an end to the city's need to pay attention to another irrelevant death. He waved the bottle. "This killed him. So did the deficiencies of diet, the parasites, exposure, congestive heart failure from bad food and lack of exercise—this man started dying the first day he landed on the streets." He turned and replaced the bottle, then brought out a small token of gold on a soiled ribbon of imperial purple. Lucaz recognized the medal.

"The Star of Valor," the coroner said. "He fought against the *Janeiristas* in '77. To die like this, a veteran . . ." He shook his head. "We're lucky, you and I. If a man who could win one of these could die like that, what might have happened to us?"

"Nothing worse," Lucaz said. He sighed. It was late, and there was nothing more to be seen there. He could get the derelict's name, if anyone could find it, from the coroner's office in the morning. It was time to go.

He turned for one last look at the scene before he buttoned up the coupe. The city ambulance was pulling away from the base of the ship. The port police were climbing back into their floater. A light showed briefly, high up on the flank of the ship, a hatch opening. A single figure stood silhouetted there, only for a moment, looking down on the police and the ambulance bearing away the corpse, and then the light was gone, the hatch closed.

Lucaz put the coupe in gear and pulled away, already composing his lead.

The ship looked like any one of a dozen such vessels docked at Turnaround's freight locks. She was an old-style fusion/magnetics brig, with its slender passenger and command hull driven lengthwise through the thicker lozenge that housed the cargo holds and the pinch-bottle generators for the fusion drives. Long since rendered "obsolete" by the new generation of reactionless agrav carriers, old split-drive intrasystem tramps such as this one still saw widespread use in the outlying colonies and by smaller importers dealing in constant-demand bulk items such as rare earths or metals.

The *Medusa's Locks* gave every impression of being just such a tramp. Her permalloy hull was scarred and pitted by the freefalling detritus of a score of star systems. Her markings were bleached and faded by the searing intensity of twenty suns. Offloading tubes had fastened leechlike over her cargo hatches, siphoning off her stocks of rare earths. These were destined for immediate transshipment to the orbital factories that would turn them into the macroscale integration circuits at the heart of the microwave traceries that laced North America and all the Earth together.

The ship looked seedy, although the grace of her lines was still clear beneath the wear. She looked as if she had never quite received the *really* thorough overhaul any good piece of machinery demands from time to time. But that was the way she was meant to look.

The *Medusa's Locks* maintained complete copies of her lines and structural blueprints in her memory banks, as naval law required, open to inspection by any authorized party. Pop the access plates set into her inner bulkheads and all the bracing and wiring would match what the plans called for—all the bracing and wiring that could be seen. Scan the unresisting ship from a distance. Nothing would be found that didn't belong. Some very smart little tricks and systems saw to that. There were strips of unusually dense metallic foil that gave off scanner shadows of structural beams that weren't where they were supposed to be. There were sophisticated electronic units that hid those beams' true locations and the things that lay concealed in their place.

A split-drive tramp shouldn't have sported such tricks and systems. It shouldn't have carried the devices those tricks and systems hid, either. Like the four smart-missile batteries located high and low, fore and aft, just beneath her hull. Like the high-energy laser whose exciter rod ran three-quarters the length of the ship, from the fusion plant to the aiming/collimating mirrors set above and below just abaft the bow. No ore tramp needed ordnance like that.

But a Guild courier did.

When humanity burst out into the stars, all the myriad assorted forms and faiths distilled from six thousand years of social experimentation went along. And so did the Guild, to do on the colony worlds what it had done on Earth, to serve as unseen and unswayable arbiter of all the creeds and movements that sought to dictate why and how men should live. So the *Medusa's Locks* and a dozen other intrasystem tramps shuttled from system to system, clinging to the great starliners like remoras to a shark, maintaining a tenuous link between the Guild and its distant branches. It was not an efficient system. Even with faster-than-light travel, news was always months or years old by the time it reached its destination. But it was the best system there was, the only system anyone had, and so it worked.

Andrea Kan Hei was not a happy woman. She could never relax whenever the *Locks* made one of its scheduled stops in Sol System under her command. Out in the colonies, her ship was as good a ship as there was, as fast and able as anything the government had out there and sufficiently well-armed to deal with a customs boat or reserve corvette if the need arose. But back in Sol System, she was an outdated design, hopelessly outclassed by the new agrav naval vessels, with nowhere to run. Her only safety lay in the security of her anonymity—and there was no way of knowing if that had been breached until it was too late.

So Andrea Kan Hei worried, from the moment the *Medusa's Locks* uncoupled from the starliner all through the long wait for an outbound starliner and a new voyage. And there was never any point at which she could stop worrying. There was always that niggling paranoid awareness born of living outside the law, that unvoiced fear that *they knew*, and were simply waiting, to see who else they could catch or for the right moment to act or for whatever unguessable reason waiting might suit them. Stopovers in Sol were just a bad time, pure and simple—and this one was worse than any, because there was no end to it in sight.

It was the Dwarf's fault, she knew that. The Guild was only exercising a sensible caution. Dani, Andrea, and her ship were the only Guild elements exposed to Óin so far, and thus the only Guild elements vulnerable to him. It was only wise not to risk further involvement. But that wisdom left Andrea Kan Hei in limbo, and she hated it, and hated Óin for his complication of her life.

A telltale on her cabin terminal lit up and buzzed as someone entered the ship's main personnel lock. The terminal's screen flashed its notification of challenge and follow-up upgrading of the ship's internal security systems. Andrea turned to her terminal and punched out the command for the lock monitor. The alert notice vanished from the screen, to be replaced by a video image of Dani and the Dwarf standing in the lock chamber, waiting to be admitted. Andrea opened her intercom.

"Good, you found him," she said. Two faces turned to look up in the direction of the speaker.

"He wasn't hiding," Dani answered.

Pity, Andrea Kan Hei thought. We'd have had an excuse for losing him then. "All right. Come on in."

Chapter Six

━━━━━━━━━━━━━━━━━━━━━━━━━━━━━━━━━━━━━━━

He looked down, Lucaz typed, *but what did he see? What could he see, from so high atop his shining machine? What could he understand? Nothing but other machines—floater, ambulance, flashing lights. There was nothing else to interest him there; what concern of his could it have been—should it have been—that some nameless vagrant had died at the base of his ship? It was not his fault; no one can say it was. He had never taken food from the dead man's hands or refused him a job or forced cheap rum down his throat. And we cannot blame him for his lack of curiosity—to work aboard one of the great ships entails many heavy responsibilities; he may even have been the captain himself, ultimately accountable for the final safety of that entire vessel and all who sailed in her.*

No. Whoever that man was, he cannot be blamed for taking so little interest in the death of one anonymous derelict.

But he was not anonymous. His name was Jorgé Angèl Amado, and he won the Star of Valor fighting to take the capital back from the Janeiristas in June of 2277 and he died of simple malaria at the foot of an antigravity spaceship. I just thought someone should know.

Lucaz sat back and stared at the screen, reading over the finished page before transferring it into storage.

Finished. One more chapter in the works of Lucaz Santiago, the lionized crusader for the downtrodden southern hemisphere. A new entry to be wired off and sold and added to the numbered opera in their elaborately bound author's display copies, racked a dozen volumes thick on the shelf above him. The new typer was a wonderful machine, a flat, compact unit that was as convenient to use propped in his lap on a shuttle flight as it was at his desk. It had been a gift from his new editor, who had been astonished to learn that he had assembled his first six collections on a primitive, fifth-hand system the size of a suitcase that actually used *bubble memory*—how positively archaic!

The new unit was entirely self-contained, would run forever, if he only exposed its diminutive photocell to afternoon sunshine once a month or so, and had room enough in its intricate, but user-transparent, light-lattice storage memory for his entire career's literary output with room for as much again. It would correct his spelling (his weak point), inspect his grammar, compute his royalties, prepare his taxes, and assemble his cover letter for him. A touch of his finger and he could quote any passage of any length from any of his last nine years' work, if he was feeling sufficiently narcissistic to refer back to his own creations.

It contained a versatile dictionary, a competent thesaurus, and could translate his work automatically into any of the eight major regional tongues. The only thing it couldn't do, *Dio Gracias*, was add a single new word of its own. Another triumph of the indomitable human nature, Santiago thought wryly. A pity the cybernetic lout didn't know when it was beaten. He felt a little peculiar using it, still, writing of dead, vagrant war heroes and other denizens of the streets of Brasilia on a neat, efficient, clickabeeping triumph of Northern science. Digital pathos? Data-flow tragedy? An incongruity, perhaps, but no more so than Lucaz Santiago himself, surely, seated in ample comfort within the latest model executive's float chair, amid the climate-controlled opulence of his suite in one of Brasilia's most exclusive residential towers, more than a quarter of a mile above the very streets that had shaped him and the work he wrote.

He felt a small pang of guilt, the same one he felt every time the irony of his position was brought home to him. That he, no longer poor, no longer faceless, far from it, should be considered the spokesman and advocate of those streets he had left behind seemed at times absurd. But then the pang would pass. If he had left those streets behind, it was because he had climbed up out of them himself. If all the others, all the Jorgé Angèl Amados he had known had not or could not, for want of exploitable talent or strength or simple lack of a chance, follow him, then he would drag them up behind him singlehandedly, if need be. Half a world was denied the heritage of the stars out of simple historical inertia, and the anger of that realization could still burn as hotly in his breast as on the first day he had discovered it. The North could pay for Lucaz Santiago's words with their money and their floater chairs and their suites and their praise—they could never meet the price of his heart.

He swiveled his chair to the phone. He tapped out a name, and a section of the suite's wall seemed to dissolve as the holoblock took shape, offering him a view of the skyline from High New York and the face of his agent.

Tobias Landon was known to be one of the toughest in the business. He always had been, even in the days before he had caught hold of a hot Latin skyrocket named Lucaz Santiago and ridden him to the top, but now he had the client list and the accomplishments and the income to prove it. He could look the most penurious syndicator in the eye, slap down the most arrogant, meddling packager, and get the deal he wanted, when he wanted, how he wanted.

He looked at Lucaz and went pale.

"Oh, it's you."

"I'm glad you're so happy to see me," Lucaz said.

"Yeah, well." It hung there until it was obvious that that was all he meant to say.

"Tobias, what is the matter? It is three weeks yet to my deadline, and I have the package finished. You are going to be even richer, sooner. Why are you so upset?"

Landon hesitated and then blurted it out. "I can't take the package, Lucaz."

"What?"

"I can't take *anything* from you anymore. Transplanet's backing out of the deal."

"*Why?* This is impossible! What are you crazy Nortés doing up there?"

"Nobody is going to touch you anymore, Lucaz." Landon seemed to steel himself. "You're on the list."

"What? What list?"

Landon looked out at him, frightened and angry. Whatever it is, Lucaz thought, he does not wish to be involved in it.

"What list?" Landon repeated. "*The* list. The *List*. The *Guild* list."

"The Guild—Jesus and Mary." The room suddenly seemed thin and insubstantial around him. "Why?"

"It's the goddamned Guild; how the hell do I know why? I don't want to know why. I'm sorry, man, but right now I don't even want to know you."

"What the devil am I supposed to do?" Lucaz asked him.

"I don't know. I don't want to know. For all I know, I'm sinking deeper and deeper just talking to you like this. I'm sorry, man. I'm out." He hesitated, as though something wouldn't let him cut the connection. "Get to the Confederacy. Forget the locals; they can't buck the Guild. Go to the top."

"Tobias—"

"No more, man. Sorry." The holoblock evaporated, a ghost of Tobias Landon staring briefly out at him before vanishing, too. Lucaz tapped out his number again and got a flashing "Not Available" notice.

Lucaz keyed off his chair and stood, pacing agitatedly across the suite. Then, suddenly, he became acutely aware of the large bay window taking up the outer wall. He saw nothing but blue sky and rooftops, but that was all he *saw*. The bedroom seemed like a much better place to think things over. No windows.

The Guild. Why? Why him? Lucaz wondered. But he knew it was pointless to speculate. If the Guild could be comprehended, the Guild could be dealt with—and no one had managed to do that yet. Lucaz doubted that he would find the trick of it in the little time he had—if he had any time at all. How long could it take the Guild to come for him? How long ago might they already have *started*?

He had to get out of the suite. It would be the first place they would come. He would have to run. But where? He dismissed Landon's suggestion that he turn to the Confederacy for protection; it couldn't even protect its own members when it wanted to, not from the Guild—and how hard would it try to shield some petty journalistic gadfly who had grown fat attacking it?

No, he had nowhere to run to—so that was where he would go.

He hastily packed a travelsac of spare clothing—the older, plainer stuff from his hungry days. He hesitated at taking anything else, even his author's copies: too much to carry, and they would do him no good. But he took the typer. That part of his life he would not be driven from.

Then he took the express lift down to the lobby of the tower, stepped through the doors, and vanished into the streets that had made him.

The grubby little hotel (*"Transients/Permanents/ State Aid Credits Accepted"*) faced off one of the labyrinthine side-streets laced serpentlike around the broad promenades of the moneyed district. There the sidewalks were never so immaculately clean as they were around the towers, or as well lit at night. There the old stone walls of the buildings were still streaked with dirt and cooking-smoke from hundreds of old, cheap open-flame stoves. The signs in the barred windows of the small stores were crudely printed in the traditional Portuguese rather than the trendy Terric of the towers, and the people were as shadowed and inward-turning as the narrow strips of pavement they walked.

Lucaz's room, complete with "kitchen"—a two-burner stove set by the sink—and a solid bed, an actual frame with old-fashioned padding, was costing him infinitely more than it was worth, and three times the hotel's posted rate. The *hosteliero* had not recognized him but with that same carnivorous, streetwise instinct for the opening, for the vulnerable, that had propelled Lucaz up from just such a room as this, knew a man on the run when he saw one. It was as though the nine years of his life since he first began writing stringer copy for the North American syndicates had been stripped away, throwing him back to the days in the streets when the promise of a room such as this to return to seemed the height of success.

Very well, then, Lucaz thought. He was back to those days. If he had lived through them once, he could survive them again. At least this time he had the advantage of money: to have had to fight the Guild and hunger as well would have been to confront too great a foe. He would have to exercise caution in tapping his accounts. He would make a point of drawing his funds from cash outlets all over the city. He had no way of knowing whether or not the Guild could access the credit network's transaction records, so he would proceed on the assumption that it could and bless his good fortune that he had not been caught in the North, where cash money had long since been superceded entirely by the credit network.

He had to laugh. How quickly the old habits and ways of thinking came back, how readily he returned to the philosophy he had labored for nine years to be able to afford to put aside. Be satisfied with a place, anyplace, to spend the night; anything you don't know about will probably hurt you; hide the source of your money.

. . . How many young men had he known just like that, in the streets? How many years had he been such a man, living in the streets but not part *of* them, not part of the community he moved through and acted on or against? That had been such a great part of his anger; then, the half-formed suspicion that there was something going on of which he was no part and could not profit from—and now he was back there again. This time, though, he knew there was such a something, because he had lived in it for nine years before a frightened man had exiled him again with a phone call. *That* hurt, that rejection, all the more so because it brought home to Lucaz Santiago how thoroughly he had been seduced by the culture above which he had thought he set himself, as critic.

The lionizing, the fame, yes, and the wealth: he had accepted the duplicitous testimony of all those things as proof that Lucaz Santiago mattered, that he was after nine years somewhat more essential to the orderly proceeding of the universe than he had been as a hungry slum child. Now he had learned better, or relearned what he had half-forgotten. Lucaz Santiago mattered to Lucaz Santiago, no one else. His *product* mattered to Tobias Landon and the syndicates, his leverage as a public figure mattered to the people he supported, but he himself, not a whit. Tobias would find other clients, the southern hemisphere activists would find another spokesman, and the death or survival of Lucaz Santiago would be a matter of convenience and nothing more. Except to himself. . . .

"I will not tolerate this!" Andrea Kan Hei raged.

"I don't see what you can do about it," Dani said.

"Three weeks! Three weeks we've sat here, waiting for the Guild to make up its mind! Three weeks, doing nothing."

"That's not entirely the case," Óin said.

"I don't consider moving from dockside to a parking orbit a significant change in our condition."

"We don't have a condition," Dani said. "We don't

exist, remember? And until the Guild can assure itself that things will stay that way, we'll just have to keep doing nothing. Unless, of course, you have some kind of option open that I don't know about."

"Options, who has options?" Andrea asked. Óin, sitting catty-corner at one end of the *Locks'* cramped wardroom, seeming to take up at least half of what little space there was, laughed quietly.

"Do you find that amusing?" Andrea demanded.

"Not at all," Óin assured her, three-fingered hands spread placatingly. "I sympathize entirely."

"They're not in any rush," Dani said. "No reason they should be. The longer they can leave us just falling in circles up here without taking any action at all, the longer they're absolutely safe. No involvement, no risk." It was her turn to chuckle. "Maybe that will be our greatest contribution to the common good, just drifting around up here forever; save somebody on high the trouble of dictating a memorandum."

"They'd never do that. They'd never abandon us."

"Well, no, I don't suppose they would," Dani said. "I'm sure they'll send us food every now and then, maybe even a bottle of new air once in a while. I'm partial to Lucerne Spring myself—excellent bouquet, a bit stuffy, perhaps, but still. . . ."

"I'm astonished at your attitude," Andrea reproved her. "How can you simply sit there and joke about this. I don't think you realize our vulnerability, how tenuous our position here is—"

"I realize all of those things," Dani said wearily. "Believe me, I know just how vulnerable we are. I think I even understand what your situation is. There just aren't many places to run up here. But I also know that we can't do a damn thing until we get instructions, so complaining to each other isn't going to do us a damn bit of good. We'll be taken care of, captain, you know that."

"This is *his* fault, you know," Andrea groused.

Óin looked at the two of them. "Did I leave the room?"

"It's not his fault—" Dani began.

"Yes, it is," Andrea said. "His, and yours. Why did you have to bring in an outsider? Look at the trouble it's caused."

Óin sighed. "First I'm not here, and now I'm an it." He made a great show of knitting his fingers together and looking upward to the bulkhead.

"That's not what she meant," Dani said, and then, to Andrea, "I brought him in because I needed him, or I would have missed my subject. I brought him in to get a job done."

"It was a violation of our every procedure. No wonder it's caused such confusion. There's a way things should be done, a way things should be—"

"I'm not much for 'shoulds,'" Dani said. "I needed Óin to get my subject, so I brought him in. I can't do anything now until the Guild sends us instructions, so I won't fuss about it until then. I let my situations make my choices; they work better that way. I'm a big believer in that."

"I'd noticed," Óin said.

Chapter Seven

Lucaz knew he was being stalked.

He had kept to his policy of drawing his money from cash outlets in different neighborhoods at random to minimize the risk of his being tracked down by his withdrawals. After several trips to all parts of the city, he had realized that the one outlet he had not utilized was the one not ten blocks from his rooms. In a feeling of intense paranoia, he had dutifully stopped there that day to make sure they couldn't find him by determining which outlet he was ignoring.

And now someone was following him.

Lucaz quickened his pace, knowing that he could not return to his room, not now. He had looked back, once, and not seen anything; now his back felt naked, exposed, the thin fabric of his tunic no defense against the death he imagined drawing up behind him.

Lucaz was unarmed. He had made that decision his first day in hiding. With his ample funds, he knew he would have no trouble securing an illicit weapon through the market of the streets, but he would not. He remembered the last time he had used a weapon on another man. It had been a gang thing, a matter of youthful pride overheated by summer nights and Rio beer. It had been an affair of cheap knives and clumsy brawling over a matter half-forgotten before the fight even began. And when it was over Lucaz stood, "victorious," his hands and forearms bleeding and etched with the cuts that still scarred them today, while his enemy, no, the youth he had fought, rolled around on the sidewalk, doubled over, a four-inch cut in his belly. Lucaz had known he could not do that again. Perhaps that had even been the moment when he decided he had to climb out of the streets. If he could not play by the rules, he didn't belong in the game.

But now someone was stalking him. He didn't have a weapon. He had no place to run. There was nothing he could do—

He heard footsteps now, light, padding, the merest scuffing of shoes on pavement. Lucaz quickened his pace. *Dios*, no, he thought, please, why, I never did anything to you—

The footsteps behind him stutter/skipped. Something grabbed at his shoulder. Lucaz Santiago screamed.

He whirled around, swinging blindly, not thinking. He felt his fist strike something yielding, and he swung again, lunging, consumed by fear and and inchoate aggression. He blundered into his assailant, and they both fell back. Lucaz felt impacts on his back and shoulder. He ignored them, punching wildly. He caught a glimpse of something metallic and grabbed for it. Pain burned in his hand, but he held on.

He drew back his other fist for a blow with all his weight behind it, and he found himself staring, fist cocked, into the eyes of the young boy whose chest he was sitting on. The youth was staring back up at him, just as afraid and wildly angry as Lucaz. He was still swinging at him ineffectually with his free hand, sloppy, powerless hooks at Lucaz's head and shoulder. Lucaz caught his fist and held it, looking down.

The boy was all of sixteen, if that, with the whipcord definition of street-life, and a thick shock of lank black hair that fell into his eyes as he looked back up at Lucaz. One cheek was bruised and swollen where Lucaz had first punched him. He wore a cheap synthetic shirt of glaring scarlet and yellow in just the sort of adolescent bad taste Lucaz would have favored himself. And he was no more a Guildsman than Lucaz Santiago.

Lucaz looked over and saw why his other hand was still paining him. The boy had a knife, and Lucaz, grabbing for it, had taken the base of the blade in the web of his thumb. He shifted his grip and pulled the knife from his attacker's hand.

"What do you think you're doing?" Lucaz demanded, brandishing the knife. "*Hé, pachucito,* what is this?" The youth didn't answer. Lucaz shifted his weight onto the balls of his feet and rose, then dropped his weight heavily back onto the boy's chest. "Talk to me!"

"I saw you at the money-box!" the boy gasped. Lucaz stared at him briefly, then cursed and twisted off his chest. He sagged back against the grimy wall of the building, while the boy sat up stiffly and rubbed his abused ribs. Neither of them moved farther, though the boy kept his eyes on the knife in Lucaz's hand.

Perfect, he thought disgustedly. He had been so utterly terrified of the almighty Guild hunting him down that he had forgotten the common-sense precaution of not flashing cash on the street. Of course the boy had come after him. Who wouldn't have tried to take such an obvious mark? It was Lucaz's own damn fault if it was anybody's. He had set himself up. It would have served him right to get robbed.

And for all his high-principles, the first thing he had done had been to pound the boy into the pavement.

Lucaz dug into his pocket and pulled out a handful of the bills he had received from the machine. He threw them onto the sidewalk by the boy.

"Take it and get out of here," he said. "Go on."

The boy reached for the money and hesitated, looking at Lucaz, at the knife.

"*Vaya!*" Lucaz snapped, and raised the blade. The boy grabbed at the crumpled bills and fled.

Lucaz looked at the weapon, with its cheap, shiny blade and fake mother-of-pearl grips, and tossed it away with another curse. He didn't need a weapon; he needed a keeper.

Then he heard the new footsteps and looked up.

Two men stood there in immaculate civilian clothes far too good for the neighborhood. The nearest one looked down at him through blue-gray eyes beneath a tall forehead and close-cropped, flaxen hair.

"Mister Santiago?" Impeccable northern Terric. "I'm Asper Maarten, Confederate Security Arm. We've been looking for you, sir."

The buzzer brought Dani awake instantly. She began to rise, then checked herself and rolled easily to one side, clearing the bottom of the lockers above her berth in the cramped cabin as she stood.

Andrea Kan Hei looked out of the screen at her with an expression of odd satisfaction. "Get your pet eety out of bed and get him packed."

"Why?"

"He's going to Earth."

It was a vista of permanent night. The frozen sea at the top of the world stretched away in all directions, divided from the black sky above by a thin, pale ring of light that encircled the horizon: ground light, reflected back into Earth's sky in the far distance. The weak luminance picked out stray planes and angles of ice where compression ridges had been driven up between colliding ice floes, highlighting them with a faint, nacreous radiance. It was the only natural light in the scene. The sky above the ice was unrelieved black, the stars masked away by the enormous sunshield overhead, twin to the ones above the Sahara and Antarctica, the Gobi and the Australian outback and lifeless patches of ocean in mid-Atlantic and Pacific. They slowed the accretion of solar heat in the Earth's atmosphere, retarding the melting of the ice caps and perhaps even bleeding off a little manmade warmth, putting off the day when the heartworld of the Confederacy broiled itself in its own industrial waste heat long enough for it to be someone else's problem.

But there were other lights.

The structure seemed to rise naturally out of the ice-pack, like a crystalline dagger thrust skyward by some great subterranean outburst. But where the plain surrounding the tower was ice, simple frozen seawater, the tower gleamed with the sleekness of the tough, ablative ceramic armor that covered it totally. Where the facets and angles of the ice fields were the result of natural processes working over the course of centuries, the canted faces of the tower had been designed and shaped deliberately, with utmost cunning, so that several facets covered any possible approach—and with them, the powerful battle lasers channeled through a maze of fiber-optic pathways within them.

It was an intimidating sight standing there, seemingly invincible in its fluted symmetry. And then, as Óin watched, the holoblock image was overlayed with new traceries of pale light between the warning pylons with their scarlet beacons. Refraction fields, cousin in principle to the sunshields, that could turn any incoming laser. Fields of directed electromagnetics meant to fend off material assault. Delicate energies that could warn the denizens of the tower against anything that approached them. It was an impressive system, known in such detail only from the incomplete reports of the six Guildsmen who had gone against it and not returned.

"And now they wish to send me," Óin said.

"That's the idea."

"What makes this a task for me? Are there no Guildsmen on Terra?"

"You're a Guildsman on Terra," Dani said, ignoring the look Óin gave her, "and yes, there are. But this is a special case. Regular Guildsmen—human Guildsmen— can't cope with that system. But you can take a human Guildsman. Maybe you can handle the tower, as well."

"That seems valid enough reasoning," Óin said, his

face expressionless. "But it doesn't get me started back home, does it now?"

"No, it doesn't," Dani admitted. She held his stare through a long silence.

"You're waiting for something," Óin said. "What?"

"For you," Dani said. "You're taking this too damned calmly."

"And how would you think I should take it?"

"I don't know. If you'd asked me that three weeks ago, I would have thought I had an answer, but . . . there's too much about you I'm not aware of. Here you've just been told that we're going to break our promise to send you home and use you as an assassin again, and—I don't know. I would have thought you'd be angry. I thought you'd bellow and roar and maybe even bend some furniture. But you're not doing any of those things. So what *are* you doing?"

"I'm accepting the command of those with whom I have taken service."

"But it wasn't the command you wanted to hear. And it isn't what we promised you," Dani said.

"It was a lawful order nonetheless," Óin said. "I took service with your Guild. Knowingly or not, wisely or not, rightly or not, I took your service, and that is what is. Having taken your service, I must take your orders; given an order, I must carry it out. There is nothing else I can with honor do."

"Will that count in your favor back home?" Dani asked.

Óin's expression hardened. "Nothing will count in my favor at home anymore. But it counts in my favor with me. I am ruined—there is no truth for me past that—but at least I may still conduct myself correctly in my disgrace."

"That could be more than we've done by you."

"And should that make a difference? My honor, such as is left of it, isn't something to be bartered as though it were trade goods, a measure of mine for a like amount of your own. I have taken your service. Honor, my honor,

109

which I owe to myself if to no one else, dictates that I obey those I am pledged to. How your Guild conducts itself, how you might conduct yourself, is your own affair. It changes nothing of my obligations. Send me to Earth, send me to this tower, send me for this Santiago. I will go."

"That must be a hell of a hard attitude to live by," Dani said.

Óin grinned bleakly. "I must confess, for me it has been made easy. What can happen to me if I do not?"

"That's true, I suppose."

"There is, however, a condition. . . ."

"You had us worried," the quiet voice said.

Dani Yuen sat carefully upright in the small lounge, sure she was being monitored visually as well as audibly, paying close attention to the potential treacheries of body language.

"Why?" she asked, looking toward the small speaker on the end table, source of the voice.

"You did virtually everything but order him to refuse us. That was certainly a rather liberal interpretation of our request that you ascertain his state of mind."

"He didn't."

"No thanks to you," the voice said unemotionally. "We have no idea why he took this so calmly. No Terran human would have."

"No Terran human has ever needed to," Dani answered. "The Guild has never used outsiders before. It's never been our way, never. We've always been responsible for our own affairs."

"You changed that."

"I know. And look what it's done."

"And you should understand the imperative behind it. We have never needed outsiders before. This time we do."

"Why?"

"Because this new Security Arm facility is something beyond us. That cannot be allowed to continue. We must maintain the impression of our efficacy."

"So that makes it all right? Let's suborn an unwilling agent, let's coerce a free being into doing our work for us whether he believes in it or not? After all, it's to our benefit. It's necessary." Dani leaned forward. "The last person I heard voice that opinion I was ordered to kill."

"You let your idealism get the better of you," the voice chided gently. "Yes, that is a philosophy we exist to oppose. But you must understand enough of our way to realize that we may only oppose it by embracing it. After all, what is assassination but the ultimate coercion? What can more totally imprison a free being than death? You sit here and object to the fundamental dichotomy that we all must live with: that we are what we resist. We feel for you if you have never realized that this dichotomy exists before now—but we must think less of you if you cannot see the difference between us and those we act against."

"Perhaps you'd best explain that difference to me," Dani said. "I'm not certain I could recognize it anymore."

"The difference is simple. We know when to stop. We grant all the prerogative to live their own lives—to that point where they threaten that prerogative in others and no farther."

"And isn't that the prerogative that the Guild is denying Óin Ceiragh?"

"Absolutely. Just as you did on Wolkenheim, when you deceived him about your own loyalties and then put him in a position where he would have to kill your subject for you."

"Don't you think I'm aware of that?" Dani asked quietly.

"We know you are aware of it," the voice said. "It is all we have been talking about. You are not worried about our accountability; you are worried about your own. We wish there was some reason we could tell you you need not feel this way, but we cannot. There isn't.

The Guild has wronged Óin Ceiragh. You have wronged Óin Ceiragh. The only excuse we may make is that it had to be done."

"And is that any excuse at all?" Dani asked.

"It must be. Otherwise, there is nothing to do but do nothing. We do not think you as a Guildswoman can want that."

"As a Guildswoman?" Dani shook her head. "No, I don't think I can, either."

"It may yet be unnecessary. We have other approaches against the tower yet untried. But Óin Ceiragh must be ready."

"He will be," Dani promised. "But there is a condition. . . ."

The room was small, no larger than the cramped cabins aboard the *Medusa's Locks*, and lacked all furnishings save for the bed and the spartan ablutory. It was not a place for living in: it was merely a box, a place to hold people until other people in other rooms were ready to receive them.

It seemed to Óin Ceiragh that his entire life had been reduced to a series of such boxes. Boxes like ship cabins, human and Basiri, always too high-ceilinged and never really wide enough to be comfortable, designed in sensible, durable metals and synthetics that could never do more than approximate good leather and wood and stone. And the ships themselves, from battered Terran tramps up to the vast Consortium Cities Mercantile: whatever their design or world of origin, they were all the same to Óin, boxes of incomprehensible complexity that bore him from star to star and year to year, all beyond his control.

There were other boxes, subtler boxes, as well— boxes of choice stacked one within the other like some elaborate Basiri child's toy, so that climbing out of one only left him in another, wider and deeper than the first. He had taken Basiri service to escape the Galatian box of choice that otherwise condemned him to a life of futility as the tolerated younger son of a *baredan*. As such, he would never know status or prestige or power save by reflection from those above him. But the Basiri box had been no improvement, only a change. It was honorable service, but it was petty service: the battles he fought were little more than extensions of merchants' bickerings, fought over trade disputes or payment deficits as though the Basiri and the worlds they dealt with were urchins squabbling over change in a gutter. It had been a lawful allegiance but not really a creditable one, and Óin had come to fear that if he did indeed serve out the full term of his bonding, he would at its end have been fit for the society of none but the Basiri and their like, tainted by their shopkeeper's ways.

Then he had stumbled upon Dani Yuen and her rogue Guildsman, and the choice she had seemed to offer, a chance to end his service quickly and honorably, to go home a person to respect in his own right—*ai, shta*, what a box that had put him in, a box of manipulation and disgrace, a box he would never, ever be able to escape.

So more boxes didn't really matter to him: not the sealed shuttle he rode down from Turnaround to Earth, not the sterile, isolated cubicle he found himself in now, not the shame of another assassination. When one box was too vast to climb out of, there was no point in worrying about the one beyond it.

But there were still corners of his present box that he would not try to fit himself into.

The door opened, and Dani walked in.

"Did they agree?" Óin asked.

"They didn't want to," she said. "They said you've already got as much information as any Guildsman ever has before a run; that's true, you know."

"But I am not any Guildsman," Óin said. "It is not enough to know the who and how and where of this task, not for me. I must face this Santiago and kill him for your Guild. It is little enough to ask that you give me the why of it, as well. What has he done to merit killing? How does he threaten your Guild or your world or whatever it is he threatens. Is it too much to know the cause I kill for? Is it too much to know who this Santiago is and what he has done—and why?"

"Most Guildsmen wouldn't want to know their subjects as well as that."

"Perhaps most Guildsmen would rather face subjects than people. Now, will they give me what I ask for?"

"They already have," Dani said, holding up the small player. "They were ready to turn you down. I had to lead them to believe that you might become unreliable if you were refused."

"And they believed that?" Óin asked. Then he chuckled. "Ah, and why not, then? After all, I already stand marked as assassin and hypocrite; why should they not fear treachery of me into the bargain?"

"For what it's worth," Dani said, "I don't."

"I'm flattered by your confidence," Óin said, "but why don't you?"

"I'll be damned if I know." Then she grinned, as though to lessen the weight of her uncertainty for both of them. "Maybe I'm experiencing your *sgeadhanha-dan* again."

"Maybe you are." Óin left her grin unanswered.

"Well . . . In any case, I still don't believe you'd sell us out."

"Be assured, I would not." And Óin knew that was the truth, although he no longer believed he could ever make it clear to these people.

These humans thought of everything as a commercial transaction. It was implicit in their very language: "treachery into the bargain," "sell us out." They saw honor and service as business commodities, as goods to be offered or withheld for the greatest personal profit. Of course they feared treachery from him, he thought. Treachery was but the next logical step in such a relationship. If one could "sell" his commitment for personal advantage—as Óin had tried to do, disastrous-

114

ly—then there was no real barrier to violating that agreement as well for even greater benefit.

It annoyed him somewhat. He would be a loyal servant of the Guild, in whatever time was left to him. That was the only proper course left open to him, and he would follow it, dry solace though it was. He just wished he'd been granted the chance to display such nobility in front of people who might appreciate it. It would have made a fine, black song back home.

"Well," Dani said into the lengthening silence. "I'll leave you to your reading. Who knows?" She shrugged. "You might even decide he deserves it."

"Who knows?" Óin agreed. "So many of us do."

The door slid shut behind her. Óin eased back clumsily onto the edge of the bed, its fields set too high off the floor, his legs straight out before him, and began to study the man he was to murder.

Minutes later, he put the player down with the last pages unread, forgotten in the wild hope that gripped him.

Chapter Eight

▰▰▰▰▰▰▰▰▰▰▰▰▰▰▰▰▰▰▰▰▰

"They're coming again," Asper said. "Want to watch?"

"I suppose I must," Lucaz replied. "After all, they are going to all this trouble on my account."

Asper swung around at his function desk in Lucaz's apartment, tapping out commands on his keyboard. The apartment's holowall dissolved into a scene from somewhere deep in the tower, where uniformed men rushed about and bent purposefully over consoles. Asper touched another switch, and an image of a screen keyed in over the activity, glowing with a stylized representation of the landscape surrounding the tower, across which a tiny dot of light approached trailing flickering numbers.

"He's coming down fast," Asper said.

Miles above them and miles away, the Guild reentry capsule punched down into the atmosphere in a streaming torrent of flaming gas, locked in on its homing pulse.

There was renewed activity on Lucaz's holowall and the readout on the keyed screen began to hash and break up.

"Jamming," Asper commented. "I think they're serious about this."

"I would hope so," Lucaz said. "I would hate to think I was worth only a casual murder."

116

Slabs of ceramic armor pivoted aside on the face of the tower, revealing the mirrors of the lasers beneath.

"Will he make it?" Lucaz asked.

"Oh, no, sir," Asper answered. "But it's the smart move. Come in fast, right to the base of the tower. If he gets inside, we'll have trouble, but it won't come to that."

The blip representing the capsule reached the outline of the tower's perimeter fields. A thin wailing of alarms reached them through the room speakers.

"Penetration," Asper said.

The zones of directed magnetics surrounding the tower clawed at the rushing capsule, seeking a grip somewhere in its ceramic and alloy structure.

"They'll have to take it out direct," Asper said.

The aiming mirrors of the facing lasers pivoted and targeted. A scatter of rubied lances struck out from the walls of the tower into the dark sky above.

Three of them hit. The tough ceramic of the capsule had been designed to cope with the thousands of degrees of friction heat generated in atmospheric reentry, but the intense localized heat of the laser impacts overwhelmed it. The ceramic failed, breaches were poked through its featureless surface, and the capsule broke up in a burst of steam and exploding Guildsman.

Asper reached out and switched off the holowall.

"That's eight," he said.

"A waste, captain," Lucaz said.

"You have to admire their discipline, though," Asper said.

"Do I?"

"It took nerve to make a run like that, sir."

"I'm sorry, captain. But I must persist in considering discipline and nerve in the service of killing me as criminality."

"Well, yes, certainly, sir. . . ."

"Certainly, indeed. Have they agreed to my proposal to resume my writings through government channels yet?"

"I don't see any messages from up top here, sir. I'd imagine they haven't made a decision."

"But it has been nearly a month since you have brought me here!"

"These things take time, sir."

"But it makes such good sense. The Guild wants me silenced; you wish to thwart the Guild; I wish to resume my writing. What better way to show that the Guild is vulnerable than to have my work out where all can see it?"

"Just keeping you alive shows that the Guild is vulnerable, sir."

"Yes, of course, but it's not the *best* way—"

"Maybe it's all the Confederacy wants of you."

"What do you mean?" Lucaz asked.

"Well, sir, please understand that this is all pure speculation on my part, that's all, but you have to admit that you were something of an agitator, at least in the Confederacy's eyes."

"I was against starving people. I've never been able to understand what made that such a dangerous position."

"I'm sure I don't know myself, sir. But you have caused something of a stir a few times."

"And?"

"So, I can imagine somebody up top deciding that they need you alive to hurt the Guild, but there's no reason they should help you make trouble for *them*, sir."

"Then what is the point of keeping me alive at all?"

"Because it's the Guild that wants you dead, sir. That's what takes priority in this case."

"I see. What is your position on this, captain?"

"Captains don't have positions, sir. There's no space for them on our monthly efficiency reports."

"Of course." Lucaz sighed. "So it will continue. The Guild tries to kill me for whatever reason I threaten them. The Confederacy protects me to spite the Guild but won't let me publish for fear of upsetting their precious status quo, which effectively does the Guild's job for them, and only Lucaz Santiago loses. If I were a morbid man, captain, I might say I would welcome my assassination. At least it would be a resolution."

"We'll kill a good few more of them before then, sir."

"Of course you will. You'll kill them, they'll kill you, perhaps they'll kill me, perhaps you'll kill my career. So much killing. It becomes difficult to tell the healing cauterization from simple pyromania."

"As long as you're not the one burning, sir. Maybe you should settle for that."

"Yes, perhaps I should," Lucaz agreed wearily. "So many of us do."

Óin hung suspended within the bed as the symbioplast grew.

He drifted gently back and forth in the suspensor field, the skeleton harness of Guild assassin's armor locked cruciform about his limbs and torso. The immature coils of woven symbioplast "muscle" were anchored firmly at the base points of the harness. Feeding on the growth stock pumped in from overhead, the strands inched outward over joints and sockets, submerging flesh and metal and inert circuitry in their spread. The kinesthetic educational inputs told him that he would remain suspended that way, locked rigid in the unpowered exoskeleton, until the coils had finished their growth and the tough ceramic overskin could be applied.

Until then, Óin could only drift, isolated, cut off from the world by the walls around him, cut off from the floor by the bed's agrav suspensor field, cut off even from his own body by the educational inputs that controlled his limbs. His arms, his hands and his legs twitched minutely from time to time as the Guild teaching machines flooded his mind with artificial memories of the weapon growing around him. The only thing they did not deprive him of was his consciousness. As their machines shaped his body to the Guild's ends, he was free to stare at the ceiling and remember.

Symmetry Fair and Wolkenheim had been shaped for humans, never for *gal-adheni* Dwarves. His appetites had been too excessive, his enthusiasms too vigorous, his sheer physical strength too dangerous. He had alarmed them, or amused them, and when he was not careful, he had injured them.

But it had never occurred to him to accommodate them, he thought now. He had been Óin Ceiragh, a *gal-adheni* doing mercenary service with the Basiri Consortium Mercantile, selling his strength for a future back home. When they had not accepted him as that, he had simply withdrawn from them, insulating himself in drink and self-righteous self-pity.

Then he met Dani Yuen as the defecting Guildsman she hunted tried to kill her—and Óin, for convenience' sake.

He should have left it at that after his first fortunate escape. But there was Dani Yuen, her partner killed, herself facing an armored and trained assassin, ready to go out after him again.

Such unquestioning acceptance of an onerous task would have won vows of comradeship and fealty in any clan-hall back home, and so Óin had instantly declared himself her ally. . . .

But of course he wasn't back home, and she hadn't been *gal-adheni*. She was a human and an assassin, and because Óin had not realized these things, he had trapped himself in his arrogant perspective. He had wrongly looked on Dani and the Basiri and the whole universe he had wandered through so blindly as flawed *gal-adheni*, never as creatures in their own right.

Now he paid.

He heard the door open and tried to look and see who had entered. He couldn't. The collar of the armor held his head rigidly in place. Nothing could be permitted to interfere with the proper growth of the symbioplast.

There was a suggestion of movement by his side.

120

Then Dani Yuen was looking down at him, her face shadowed by her long hair.

"Comfortable?" she asked.

"As if I were drifting on air."

"It shouldn't be much longer. They tell me you're taking the instructions well." That was true; he was. At least the ones he chose to acknowledge.

"So," she continued, "did it help?"

"Did what help?"

"The information, about Santiago. Did it help?"

"Ah. Do you mean, did it help me decide to rejoice in being an assassin? To acknowledge the rightness of killing in stealth, out of fear? To believe that this Santiago merits black murder? I'm afraid it did not. But I did appreciate it. I felt I should at least know him before I sought his life."

"And do you know him?"

"Better than I did," Óin said. "As well as I ever will, I suppose."

"Does it make a difference?" Her expression was unreadable behind the curtain of her hair.

Óin sighed. He would have shrugged if he could. "For me. I had too much of killing strangers when I served the Basiri. We slew each other with much more familiarity back home. I felt I should return to that."

"But Santiago won't know you."

"That's not to be helped. Besides, perhaps I'll get a chance to introduce myself."

"I doubt it." He'd have enough to do staying alive, she thought. Then she wondered if there was any reason he should try. Extracting Óin from the tower after his mission was a nice idea, with, at best, a tenuous connection to immediate reality. Dani wonder if he knew that.

Then she wondered if he cared.

He had gained weight, she saw. The planes and angles of his body had become softened by a layer of fat, carbohydrates his system had failed to burn off in the Terran gravity, lighter by half than that of his home. It was not a loss of condition. It was simply a result of living in the human world, a world he had not been born to inhabit. He carried the extra weight effortlessly, as easily as he ignored the subtler inputs of the kinesthetic teaching system, the ones meant to shape his attitudes and beliefs to the Guild's liking. He didn't resist them, the technician had told Dani; he simply ignored them. Now the technicians wanted to know why, and Dani was supposed to ask.

"I hope you can tolerate the inconvenience if they don't let you do things the old-fashioned family way," she said. It seemed like a good, cautious beginning.

"Oh, I shall endure," Óin said. "Even without the encouragement of your clever little machines." He rolled his eyes expressively toward the ceiling and grinned. "Did you hear that?" he called to the roof. "I'm still working for you."

"You knew." Dani managed to make the statement a question.

"*Sgeadhanha-dan* works each way," Óin said. "To know what is is to know what it makes you. I have had ample education in the reality of my situation and months to determine my place in it. I've done that, whether you believe me or not. If I am going to have any second thoughts, I will at least know whether they are mine. These were not, and so I ignored them."

"You don't seem upset."

"I've made that mistake too many times already. I am myself and my *sgeadhanha-dan* is my own. You and yours are different. If it suits you to be so afraid, then be so."

"Afraid?"

"Oh, yes. Very much so," Óin said.

"You're going to *have* to explain that," Dani said. "If not to me then to them." She gestured at the ceiling.

"I had not thought it needed explaining," he said. "Why else should one become an assassin?"

"'An assassin is the political instrument of last

122

resort,'" she quoted, just as she had on Wolkenheim so long ago.

"I remember that," Óin said, "and I remember the rest of your speech, about how the Guild righteously defends trembling humanity from polluting industrialists and mad holymen that would bury the Earth in starving babies—but how does that apply to Lucaz Santiago?"

"I'm sure that's been decided."

"Has it? What has he done? He's chided the Confederacy, demanded that they accord the southern hemisphere full off-planet participation—"

"They can't even use it."

"Can this Finland he writes about? Or the Celtic League, whatever that is?"

"The South had its chance three hundred years ago. Instead, they gouged the North for the rights to their resources and then hoarded them when things got tight—"

"So the North does the same? Are they going to run out of galaxy?"

"It's taken three centuries since then for the North, the Confederacy, to build up a working off-planet economy. Do you know what kind of chaos it would cause to redistribute it over both hemispheres?"

"So you must kill the man who suggests it be done?"

"People are beginning to listen."

"Ah, then he is dangerous, isn't he? The people really must be protected from hearing such things, whether they want to listen or not."

"That's not what we do," Dani said sharply.

"That's what it very much sounds like."

Dani shook her head. "They can't be finding this very reassuring up top."

"I can't help that. It's a good retainer's duty to challenge his lord now and again. Then it's his duty to shut up and do what he's told."

"Well, that lets me out," Dani said. "I'm not a

retainer; I'm a Guildswoman. And I wouldn't even know who to complain to, even if I wanted to."

"Of course, you'd never want to."

"I take a side. I play by its rules."

"How very wise."

"But unlikable."

"I've promised you people my service, not my approval."

"And we can't expect it?"

"You shouldn't want it, if you take a side and play by its rules."

An unseen speaker popped into life overhead.

"Operant Yuen, please report to the conference room." The announcement came from a featureless wall.

"Oh, now I've frightened them," Óin said. "You'd better go calm them down."

"I suppose I'd better."

"And one last thing."

"Yes?"

"As I've said, your way is your own, and it's not for me to judge it. But you do realize that by your terms it's foolish to leave me alive, whether I serve you or not?"

"Yes," Dani said. "Yes, I do realize that."

"That makes it unanimous, then."

"To say that we are distressed is to put it most mildly," the room said. "We are not at all happy with the attitude of Óin Ceiragh."

"I can't help that," Dani said. "As he says, all we need is his service, not his approval. His service we have. What more do you want?"

"Assurance. He has the armor now. If he were to betray us, it would be most damaging."

"How can he betray us locked in unpowered armor?"

"We must release him soon or decide we cannot."

"He can be trusted. He's had enough chances to betray us already. He didn't on Wolkenheim. He didn't

124

on the flight back. He didn't on Turnaround. I believe he's safe."

"And so the question becomes whether you are correct and whether your judgment is valid."

Dani stiffened. "Are you doubting me now?"

"You have been in constant contact with Óin Ceiragh since you first brought him to our service. You have tried to persuade him of the rightness of our existence repeatedly; we have the records. Yet he still challenges our way."

"But he obeys us."

"That is not entirely satisfactory. And it is disquieting to note that you do not find it so, operant."

"But I do," she said. "I merely accept that I cannot change it."

"Would you have done so before you met Óin Ceiragh?"

"I don't understand. The situation had never risen before. I've dealt with it now in the manner my training and my beliefs indicated."

"That is the problem. Do you still regard those beliefs as valid?"

The quiet monotone of the questions was almost as infuriating as their content.

"Why shouldn't they be?"

"Consider," the voice said. "In all the time you have dealt with Óin Ceiragh, you have not persuaded him of our way. What has this failure done to those beliefs you mention?"

"Nothing," Dani said. She repeated it, stronger. "Nothing. You say you're distressed by Óin's doubts. Do you know how I feel about yours now? I've been an operant for seven years, a good operant; you know that. You've never had cause to mistrust me before, and you know it. I've talked to Óin Ceiragh, reasoned with him, argued with him almost daily since he was coopted— since I coopted him. How long has that been, how many months? If he was going to convert me to his fine old chivalrous ways, he would have done it long since, but

125

he hasn't. Because I'm a Guildswoman. Dani Yuen is a Guildswoman, and that's all there is to be said, whether you believe it or not."

"We would like to believe that."

"Then why are you afraid to?"

"There are so many things in this world to be afraid of. That is why we exist. That is how we have survived."

"And Óin Ceiragh is not one of them," Dani said. But she wondered if she was, now. That frightened *her*. She had put so much into being a Guildswoman. What was there without it? "He can be trusted. He will go after Santiago."

"Even knowing he may not survive?"

Dani sighed. "Even hoping he may not. . . ."

Chapter Nine

⧫━⧫━⧫━⧫━⧫━⧫━⧫━⧫━⧫━⧫━⧫━⧫━⧫━⧫━⧫━⧫━⧫━⧫━

"Three this time," Asper said. The keyed insert on Lucaz's holowall showed the blips of the Guild reentry capsules rushing across the screen. "They must be trying for a saturation approach."

The drop capsules crossed the perimeter of the tower's defensive fields. Even as the penetration signal flashed, the lasers were stabbing out.

The keyed-in screen face was blanketed in a hail of glittering motes. Asper leaned forward, suddenly intent.

"Jamming and chaff," he said. "At least a capsule's worth. They'll try to push one capsule through, blind."

"Will they succeed?" Lucaz asked.

The lights suddenly dimmed.

"What is happening?" Lucaz asked.

"Power switched to the lasers," Asper explained. "They're going to pattern fire through the counter-measures."

The sky around the tower shone with a latticework of scarlet light as the massed batteries of battle lasers fired blindly in all directions, laying down a barrier of energy against a target their gunners could not see.

On the broad scene of Lucaz's holowall, technicians worked swiftly at their boards. The jamming hash fluctuated and shimmered as they struggled to compensate for it, and then the keyed-in screen was clear except

127

for the small blip that slowly expanded and then faded away, seemingly inches from the tower.

"Got him," Asper said. "He didn't clear the pattern."

"And that makes nine," Lucaz said.

Asper shook his head. "Ten. One more last night. I didn't want to wake you."

"I appreciate your consideration, captain, but I would rather you had."

"I didn't see any need, sir. You've seen it before."

"Captain, they are trying to kill *me*, and dying for it. I should at least be aware of their attempts."

"I think you're taking this a little too personally, sir," Asper said.

"How can I do that?" Lucaz demanded. "It's my murder we're talking about, and my murderers."

"But they aren't, sir, that's the point. They're Guildsmen, and you're what they call their subject. They aren't thinking about killing Lucaz Santiago. They're thinking about hitting their target. I don't see why you should feel any more involved in that sense, sir. They're Guildsmen, objects. *Our* targets."

"Of course, the problem with not being involved in that sense is that once you aren't, there's no reason to want to stop 'hitting the targets,' is there?"

Asper shrugged. "I suppose not."

"Well, if you don't mind," Lucaz said, "I believe I will cling to my involvement. Otherwise, it may prove difficult to distinguish myself from my assailants."

"It's up to you," Asper said. "Myself, I take a side, and I play by its rules. Oh"—he reached into the pocket of his tunic and brought out a small dataplac—"thanks for letting me see your stuff, but I'm afraid I found it rather slow going. I prefer lighter material personally."

"I suppose that is no surprise," Lucaz said. He reached for the dataplac just as the room trembled. A distant booming rumbled somewhere deep in the tower just before the alarms began. "What is that?"

Asper was at his desk, punching in queries.

"I guess they were smarter than I thought," he said. "You may get to take this personally yet, Mister Santiago."

"They're inside?"

"It looks that way." He opened a drawer, pulling out a belt and harness. It was uncanny the way he sounded as calm as he always had, Lucaz thought. At least he had the good grace to look scared.

"How many? Where?"

"I'm afraid I don't know yet. A lot of the internal monitors are down." He tapped in a command. Faint metallic sounds echoed hollowly from the suite's ventilators. "I've sealed this complex. We're breathing our own bottled air, separate from the base system." He drew on the belt and harness. "This suite is specially reinforced all around, sir. If you stay in here, you should be all right."

"Where are you going?" Santiago asked.

"I have to secure this floor." He opened a cabinet Santiago hadn't known was there and took out the backpack to a heavy power-weapon. He swung it over his shoulders with practiced ease, and it locked solidly into place on the harness. He plugged in the weapon itself and slung it over his shoulder, then drew out a handgun from the bottom of the cabinet and fed in a magazine. Then he hesitated and turned toward Lucaz with the pistol.

"Here." Lucaz took the pistol, looked at it. It was heavy in his hand, with a thick barrel and wide muzzle. "You've got four rounds, shaped charges. If you need it, it should work."

"It will? How?"

"Dammit." Asper took the pistol and racked the cocking arm back, then returned it to him. "Pull the trigger now and it goes off. Aim for the belly; you're almost sure to hit something." He returned to the cabinet and withdrew a visored helmet. It gave him an odd, insectlike appearance. "The foyer doors double as

an airlock. Keep them closed to anyone who isn't me."
He turned toward the doors. "Well, good luck."

"Captain Maarten." The officer turned. "I would
take it as a courtesy if you did not die on my account."

"Very kind of you, sir. I'll keep it in mind."

The door worked twice, and Lucaz was alone. He
shifted the pistol to his other hand and winced at a
sudden stab of pain. The weight of the weapon hurt his
bandaged thumb. He looked at the handgun for a long
moment, then set it down on Maarten's desk and sat
down behind it.

Óin bounced against the ice again, clumsily, as the
currents bore him toward the tower. At least he assumed
they did. He had been jettisoned from the submersible
at a point calculated to deposit him there.

Ten feet below him, the sea stretched three hundred feet down to the silty bottom, every inch of it swept
by sonar and visual scanners. Above him, through a
dozen meters of solid ice, the tower's defensive fields and
lasers fought against the three dummy capsules burning
in toward it. But where Óin drifted there was only
darkness and silence. His light, neutrally ballasted shell
matched his infrared signature to the water around him.
The irregularities of the ice shielded him from the
sweeping sonar. As long as he did not disturb the normal
flow of the currents or expend any energy, he would go
unnoticed until he reached the tower.

Unless, of course, he missed. In which case, he
thought with a wry smile, everybody's concern about his
trustworthiness would have been wasted as he went
bobbing and tumbling off beneath the Arctic Ocean.

His passive magnetoscope began to register.
Whether he was on course or not, something very large
and very metallic stood before him. The reading slowly
ticked upward in intensity, and he was banging up
solidly against the object in the blackness.

He popped the release tabs, and his shell broke
apart around him. There was a click and a brief catch in

the hiss of his respirator unit as the shell's rebreather disconnected and he went over to his own systems. The air within his helmet was thick and breathable, kept at *adhe's* pressure, comfortable for the first time since he had left the Basiris' service.

The limpet charge came free of his chest and locked in place against the wall before him. He found the trigger by touch and armed it, then moved several meters away along the curving wall. It was a shaped charge, the bulk of its force directed inward, but there was no sense in waiting around to see how well the Guild designers had done their work.

A heavy fist struck him through the symbioplast armor as the charge detonated. He started back toward the expected rupture in the wall. It took little intent on his part. He could scarcely have resisted the inrushing sea.

He struck heavily against the lip of the rupture, and then he was inside the tower. The world lit up around him as the armor's optical systems finally found some light to work with. The symbioplast musculature came to life as he fought his way upright, so that he could at least see which way the ocean bore him.

There was an obstruction ahead, a support frame jutting out from the wall. He grabbed for it with one hand and held on as the sea swirled past him. Already he could see bulkheads slamming closed down the corridor.

He activated the suit's reconnaissance circuits and used the brief respite the flooded corridor granted him to study the graphic it flashed on the inside of his visor.

That portion of the tower above sea-level was pure killing machine, as expected. There was room for little else up there save the lasers and the field generators that contributed to the tower's defense. At the base of the tower was a shielded area his sensors could not penetrate: the tower's powerplant. The lower half of the tower was crowded with machinery he took to be its submarine defenses, the launchers and sonic weapons that had killed two Guildsmen before him. But there was a

131

shielded level just above him whose purpose he could not guess at. He would search there first.

He walked ponderously down the flooded corridor to the sealed bulkhead. The seam between the doors yielded in a sudden flood of bubbling turbulence as he drove his armored hands between them, then broke open as he thrust them apart, the oversized armor amplifying his alien strength with a power no human could ever master. The flood bore him through the doors and along the corridor, toward the waiting lift shafts.

Asper found the section waiting for him by the lift-shaft lobby. The six men, armed with plasma assault weapons identical to his own, stood clustered around their noncom.

"Sir," he said as Asper joined them.

"What's the situation, sergeant?"

The man reversed his tac board and held it up for Asper's inspection. "CIC's isolated the penetration, two levels down, sir, below ice-bottom."

"Forces?"

"On this level, we're it, sir. They're trying to move reinforcements down to us, but the flooding's shut down the lifts. I've detailed a squad each to the north, south, and east shafts, as well."

"Good enough. Let's pull this squad back past the first flood-control bulkhead and set up there. Have the other squads do the same."

"Yes, sir. All right, you heard the captain. . . ."

The narrow corridors of the tower were not built for infighting. The protruding lips of the flood-control bulkhead offered some slight cover for the two prone soldiers and the standing marksmen to each side of them, but there was nothing for Asper, the sergeant, and the last trooper but to kneel out in the open, completely exposed.

"Looking forward to this, sergeant?" Asper asked.

"Hell, no, sir. Hell of a way to put in my twenty."

"Gotta go along with you there."

There was a slight buzz, and the sergeant looked to his tac board. "Bulkhead's gone, next level down. They're on their way."

"Let's be ready. . . ."

Stupid, Óin thought as he fell. He had forced open the lift shaft as the quickest way up to his target as the corridor flooded around him. It should have occurred to him that the ocean would flood *down* the three hundred feet of lift shaft before it bore him up toward the surface. Probably the only thing that had saved his life was the stubborn lift-plate below him, retreating doggedly before the press of seawater against it. Finally, the flooding had stopped, whether because the shaft had filled entirely or because the support fields of the lift-plate had reached a level of absolute incompressibility. Now Óin made his way upward again. His progress was slow at first, then gradually accelerated as the inrushing ocean began to advance upward. The tactical graphic, flashed on the inside of the visor, warned him as the mysterious shielded area grew closer, and closer still—

He reached out for the doors of the lift-shaft, checking his ascent. They would have to be waiting for him out there, one way or the other. Stealth was useless now. He pushed away from the wall to his arm's length and raised the other, wrist cocked to bring the oversized plasma gauntlet to bear. He fired—

The lift shaft doors blew away in a gout of blue flame. Asper flinched at the concussion of the explosion, then stared at the mass of writhing foam hurtling into the corridor. Almost unconsciously, he fired without aiming, without a clear target. Then the rest of the squad opened up, long streamers of cerulean energy stabbing into the approaching water.

Mistake. The front of the rushing wave erupted into a great cloud of steam, driving down on them. Asper threw up his arms before his face as it enveloped him, searing, burning. He heard the men of the squad

133

screaming around him, could not separate his own scream from theirs. A plasma charge leaped out of the cloud, cutting down the sergeant beside him even as the first of the ocean struck heavily against his legs.

Then something enormous bulked up out of the steam, an armored figure, impossibly thickset, seeming to fill the corridor as the sea broke around it without effect. Asper swung his weapon into line and fired, but the faceless golem twisted, dodging, and though blue fire splashed across his breast, he kept on coming. Asper saw the Guildsman's fist lash out, impossibly fast, striking a man aside to disappear beneath the waves around them. Then he was turning toward Asper, striking at him with an impossibly huge fist. He tried to duck, but he couldn't, and the blow caught him in the shoulder and threw him back—

The bulkhead doors were sliding shut as Óin slammed into the soldiers and through them. It was difficult to move his right arm. Ceramic and symbioplast had run and fused together in the heat of the bursting plasma charge. Lesser armor, armor scaled for a human wearer, would have failed then. Only the greater thickness of material Óin's alien physique made possible had saved him. But it had saved him.

He was alone in the corridor, save for one of the human soldiers, the one he had thrown before him in his charge, the one who had wounded him. The man was struggling feebly, stunned or injured, trying to raise his head out of the few inches of water that had rushed through the bulkhead before it had been sealed.

Óin reached down and sat him up against the wall. The fight was over, and the man was no threat. He did not see Óin, even though his eyes were open, and the unnatural way his arm hung proved his injury. Óin left him there.

There was only one door in the stretch of corridor between the sealed bulkheads he found himself in. It offered little resistance. It bent before the first blow of his bunched fists, buckled at the second, and was torn from it tracks and bent aside at the third. A lesser door just inside the first offered even less obstruction.

Óin recognized the man immediately. Santiago stared back at him, a hand weapon forgotten on the desk before him. Óin could see the man trying to make sense of him, too short, too massive, too few fingers, and too much strength.

"What *are* you?" he asked.

Óin shrugged. "A Guildsman." And he pulled off his visor.

"You're not human."

"That I am well aware of." Fierce black eyes stared back at Santiago as Óin broke the connections to his plasma gauntlets and shook them free of his hands. He saw Lucaz stare at them as they reached to his chest and started undoing the seals of the armor.

"No one ever suggested that the Guild wasn't a human thing—"

"Oh, no," Óin said sharply as the chestplate came loose in his hands. "You people take the blame for your own sins. The Guild is human."

"But you aren't."

"That was the problem, wasn't it?" He broke open the waistband of the exoskeleton and bent to undo the leg seals, unfasten the boots. He stepped free of the armor, naked and impossible. He slapped his wide stomach contentedly, grinning through his thick beard. A layer of flab shook briefly at the impact. "I'm sorry I couldn't face you in better form," he said, "but I haven't been myself lately." The comment seemed to amuse him.

There was a sudden flare of light, a wash of intense heat, an acrid stench. The armor was gone, reduced to a puddle of slag. Óin nodded. "That's that."

"Why did you do that?"

"An obligation." He gestured to the pistol on the desk before Lucaz. "Do you know how to use that?"

"Supposedly."

"You'd best take it up, then."

"I won't shoot you."

"Why not? I am Óin Ceiragh, of Clan Ceiragh, in the service of the Guild, and I have been charged to kill you. I do think you should return the favor."

"But I am not a Guildsman, and I do not kill people."

"A good answer. But don't you fear for your life?"

"Fear is the Guild's emotion. They fear me, for whatever reason, and so they send you to kill me. If I were to kill you, out of fear, then what difference would there be between the Guild and myself?"

"None, perhaps."

"Then wouldn't they have won?"

"Oh, very good," Óin said. He seemed honestly pleased. "You are making this much worth my while."

"I am happy that you are happy."

"You truly mean this? You would die for your own identity?"

"Have I a choice?"

"You might win."

"And lose in the process. Why don't we get this over with?"

"Oh, we shall. The Guild has said I must kill you. You have said why. But the how of it is my choice." He gestured. "You really should pick that up."

His hand moved toward the pistol, almost of its own volition, then stopped.

"It is a temptation, but no, thank you."

"I hope you can do this," Óin said. "It would make this much worth my while."

"For however much longer you live. You'll never get out of here."

"If you honestly will not try to kill me, then it will have been worth it. Do you know how long I've waited for a true opponent, with something to fight for?"

"Not long enough."

Óin laughed.

* * *

The pain of his ruined arm woke him like an alarm. One second blessed unconsciousness; the next, fire.

Asper looked around. It took him only a second to realize that he sat against a sealed bulkhead door and not much longer to recall the shock of the Guildsman's attack. He did not need the cold metal of the bulkhead behind him, already chilled by the frigid arctic waters, to tell him what must have happened to the rest of the squad.

He was alone. The other squads would not have made their way past the flood-control bulkheads yet, even if they had been ordered to. His weapon lay near to hand, still jacked into its powerpack. Using it as a crutch, he levered himself to his feet.

Then he saw the ruined doorway to Lucaz's suite. He felt a pang of dismay before he heard the voices, one obviously Santiago's, the other a deeper, foreign-sounding speaker.

He swung his weapon up under his one good arm and staggered toward the door.

He had never seen anything like the creature that stood facing Santiago. But he recognized the melted remains of Guild armor and made the immediate connection. Anger boiled up inside him. This one he was going to take personally.

The muzzle of the weapon clanked against the twisted door frame as he raised it. The squat creature whirled with surprising speed to face him, and his bearded face cracked into an enormous grin. Then he spun and threw himself toward Lucaz, toward Asper's charge.

"Now!" Óin cried, and the two men raised their weapons. One of them fired.

Part Three

A RETURN

Chapter Ten

"It would have worked, too," said Óin, "if he hadn't been injured. If he'd shot straight enough." Óin absently massaged the stump of his lost arm.

"What about Santiago?"

"Lucaz Santiago." Óin grinned. "A man to respect. Yes, he picked up his weapon; he was that frightened. And then he put it down, even before I got my hands—my hand—on him. He won. I couldn't change him. A *sgeadhanha-dan* to be admired."

"But you killed him."

"That was the service I had been charged with."

"What happened after that?"

Óin sighed. "The humans did everything they could to compound their error—and they succeeded. They kept me alive. They had some idea of compelling me to tell them the whole and awful truth about the Guild of Resolution, as if I knew what that truth was, and as if they had any way to compel me."

"Didn't they?"

"What were they going to do, child? Kill me?"

"True. . . ."

"Well, they questioned me until they realized I didn't have the answers they wanted or didn't care to divulge them, and then they questioned me some more, just to be stubborn about it, but in the end they decided they didn't want to risk jeopardizing their potential relationship with our people and sent me back to the Consortium."

"I thought they knew nothing about us."

"I imagine they don't. Otherwise, I rather doubt they would be terribly alarmed by the prospect of *gal-adheni* everywhere taking up their cane-knives and wood axes and marching on the Confederacy to take revenge for one *aidjiin*. Back in the Consortium, I was able to take passage home—back to *adhe*, at least—and here I am, ever since."

"Didn't you even try to go back to Ceiragh Holding?"

Óin stirred uneasily. "To what end? Everyone I had ever known was long years dead by the time I returned, and what use could these new Ceiraghim have for a disgraced ancestor, an *aidjiin*?"

"Then your outlawry was never declared," Cian realized.

"What would have been the point? I know what I am. Why subject myself to the indignity of a public denunciation?"

"Then you are not *aidjiin*."

"Haven't you been listening, child? I am *aidjiin*. My every action has made me such."

"That is not your choice to make. It is up to the clan to cast you out. You cannot abandon your name. No *gal-adheni* ever could."

"*I* have, damn you!" Óin raged. "Look around you at the glory of Óin *aidjiin*. This hovel my holding, one good arm left to defend it from anyone stupid enough to desire it, my lands a rockpile, my life dependent on Consortium coin! No fit *gal-adheni* would live so!"

"I did not say you were a fit *gal-adheni*," said Cian Canbhei. "But you are not *aidjiin*." Óin grimaced and looked to the ceiling.

"No? I am not a fit *gal-adheni*, the child says. And I am not *aidjiin*, either. Creac's eyes, am I then nothing at all?" He looked back at Cian Canbhei. "Very well, then, child, give me the benefit of your wisdom. What am I?"

"A fool. Perhaps a coward. But you certainly have too much pride left to be a proper *aidjiin*." Óin bellowed with rage and bolted to his feet. Only the crackling fire in the pit barred him from Cian Canbhei.

"A coward! You mewling *infant*! I left my home to journey among lands whole lifetimes apart!"

"Because you were afraid of what you might become if you remained within the embrace of clan and *adhe*," Cian said quietly. "Just as I am afraid." Oh, Dhein, he thought. To learn this now.

"I fought and killed an armored Guildsman empty-handed!"

"Because you feared the burden of service with the Consortium and sought a quick way out of it."

"I sought my own death in the service of assassins!"

"Because you feared to live with the knowledge of that service and its shame," Cian said.

"I've exiled myself to this, this *hole*, a cripple!"

"Because you were afraid to face the judgment of your blood and because you feared, most of all, that they might accept you back."

"*No!*"

"Yes, non-*aidjiin*. I may be everything you say I am. I may be an arrogant, cane-cutting child, a mewling infant. I may lack a Canbhei's proper courtesy. And I am certainly every bit as afraid as you are, or I would not leave my home and my family. But you know I am right in this. I called you *aidjiin* before, and I was wrong. I apologize for my insult to yourself and your blood. But you call yourself *aidjiin*, as well, and only you can make amends for that insult."

"How?" asked Óin. He seemed almost cowed.

"Return to your hold."

"I cannot do that."

"You still let your fear rule you."

"As do you. I have not yet heard you renounce your intention to take service with the Consortium."

"True," said Cian. "Perhaps you're right. But serving the Consortium is a task I have bound myself to; I

143

cannot refuse it. You are bound to nothing, and so you are lost. You have nothing by which to define yourself, no one by which to define yourself. . . ."

Dani moved easily up the steep hillside, the Consortium gravitic mesh and the strength of the armor easily overmastering the oppressive gravity of *adhe*. She moved smoothly, mechanically, the armor working with the ease born of long, unconscious habituation. But where she could move arms and legs without dissenting thought, she could not anticipate the task she faced in such a manner.

Fear, Óin had said. Fear drove the Guild, fear of change, of progress, of a world different from the world the Guild accepted as optimum. And her masters, the unseen authority she had deferred to all her life, agreed with him. They had tried to put a different face on it, to present it as a pragmatic reaction to a world full of threats—

But Óin Ceiragh had seen no threat in Lucaz Santiago, even as he went to kill him. And Dani Yuen saw no threat in Óin Ceiragh, even as she climbed the hill to bring flaming blue death into his last redoubt.

He couldn't be right, she told herself. It wasn't fear that drove the Guild, that drove Dani Yuen. It was necessity. It had to be. There had to be a true reason for the Guild's existence—or Dani Yuen's entire life was a waste, a futile joke that she had enriched by taking it seriously. The Guild did good. There was no telling how much harm it had prevented, how much harm Dani Yuen had prevented with her killings.

There was no telling. But she could tell exactly how many people she had killed. She simply couldn't discern, had never tried to discern, how to intelligently compare that with the potential damage she had forestalled. If any.

No ifs. She had done some good. She had to have, she told herself, and began to channel her fear into anger

144

at the creature that had inspired it. She was a Guilds-woman. She would do what a Guildswoman did.

The two of them looked up in astonishment as the door-curtain was torn away and flung into the night. The Guildswoman stood there, one fist extended before her and glowing with azure luminance. No one moved.

Óin spoke first. "*Aya* Yuen," he said. "Of course they would send you. This is your affair, after all."

The faceless visor hid her suprise. "How did you recognize me?" she asked, toneless through her filters.

"*Sgeadhanha-dan* is not merely a *gal-adheni* quali-ty," he answered. "I trust I should recognize yours by now."

Cian started to rise. Dani's fist swung toward him, and Óin stopped him with a word.

"No. We'd both die if she fires in here," he said, and then, to Dani, he added, "He is not involved in this. Let him leave."

"Why?"

"Because he's no threat to you. Or would the Guild countenance the death of such a complete innocent?" Dani hesitated. "You don't have to be afraid of him, *aya*."

"All right," she said, at last. She retreated back-ward, watching them through the doorway. Cian rose and followed her out, Óin behind him.

When they stepped onto the narrow, open space in front of the hut, Óin stepped out from behind the younger *gal-adheni*. Cian saw that he had brought his crossbow.

"Move away, child," Óin said. "This is no fight of yours." But Cian Canbhei stepped up beside him, the long cane-knife in his hands.

"No," said Cian. "I would not countenance an assassin of our own kind to go unchallenged among us. I will not let her act go unopposed."

"So you would disgrace yourself instead?"

Cian forced himself to keep his eyes on the armored

145

human before them. "What are you saying? She is an assassin. There is no disgrace in opposing an assassin."

"Creac's heart, child. *I'm* an assassin. Remember? Now which of us would you preserve?"

"You thought you were giving loyal service—"

"Isn't she?" Now Cian did look at him. "Your first lesson in non-*gal-adheni* honor, child. I was a loyal servant of the Guild and served them as honorably as I could, even when it meant becoming an assassin twice over. Now *Aya* Yuen serves them honorably, even when it means assassinating me. Can you oppose a loyal servant in the honorable conduct of her duty, in an affair which does not concern you?" Cian was looking from Óin beside him to the woman who meant to kill him, desperately seeking an answer in mocking eyes and a faceless visor.

"Step aside, child," Óin said gently. "Let it be."

His face a mirror of the conflicting emotions that twisted him, Cian moved jerkily aside, the knife still raised as though to ward off the both of them. Óin turned his attention back to his hunter.

"Will you kill me, then?" asked Óin.

"I have to," answered the Guildswoman.

"Does the Guild fear me that much, then?"

"I fear you that much," said Dani Yuen. "You've cost me everything I ever valued. I'm a Guildswoman, damn you, but they won't let me have that, now. I'm tainted, in their eyes, with your doubts and your damned *gal-adheni* honor. And this is the only way I can take back what's mine."

"We've spoken much of fear tonight, the child and I," said Óin. "You don't have to let it rule you. You don't have to let being a Guildswoman rule you."

"Then what have I left?" asked Dani Yuen.

"Dani Yuen, *aya*."

"There's no dividing them," said the Guildswoman.

"If you won't, no, then there isn't," said Óin. "And that leaves only the fear." As he spoke, he lunged to one side, bringing the crossbow up and loosing a quarrel—

146

But Dani Yuen was moving, too. The bolt should have split her breastbone, killing her instantly. Instead, it ripped into and along the surface of the armor, to hang spent in a blister of gouged symbioplast. Dani fired in turn, but the plasma bolt went high and wide of the one-armed *gal-adheni*, already charging with the crossbow raised as a bludgeon.

Dani reacted instantly, aiming not at the charging Óin but into the ground before him, so that blue fire splashed up in every direction, steam and boiling earth erupting with it. Óin screamed as the half-molten soil splashed his legs and belly, staggered, and fell to his knees. In the instant Dani was upon him and an armored fist rocked his head as if it were a seed-pod atop a stalk in a high wind. She struck him again, and blood spurted from his ruined nose as he toppled backward to lie helpless in the steaming, muddy ground.

Dani raised up both arms and brought the plasma gauntlets to bear. She felt the familiar touch of their conductance beams and watched the blue fire building in their muzzles—and then the fire died, and she lowered her arms, and the faceless head drooped as though ashamed, until Cian Canbhei gave the body a mighty shake and freed his knife from her armored back. Dani Yuen collapsed awkwardly to the ground and was gone, consumed in the fires of her destructive armor.

Cian knelt beside Óin, helping him to sit up. He looked ruefully at the long knife, its point visibly blunted by the resistance of the armor.

An assassin lay dead before him, while another rose, saved by his hand. And Cian knew that he had chosen to act simply to preserve the familiar. Óin was *gal-adheni*, and in the measuring of their sins and virtues between them, that had been the one thing that had tilted him against Dani Yuen. For all his shallow talk about the other races' exemption from *gal-adheni* standards, it was the measure by which Dani Yuen had forfeited her life. She was not *gal-adheni*, and so Cian had killed her. It was a scale he could never afford to use again, and yet he had used it this time without thought. For the first time his chosen course, which had always frightened him, now left him uncertain, as well.

"It almost wasn't good enough, was it?" Óin asked, wincing through the pain of his burns.

"It was proper *gal-adheni* steel," Cian answered. "It was sufficient."

He helped Óin to rise and hobble back into the hut. At Óin's direction, he unearthed a tube of Consortium-made salve that Óin assured him was sufficient to his injuries. For a long time, neither *gal-adheni* spoke, staring at the burn scars and the molten mass of plastic on the hillside.

Óin was the first to break the silence.

"So, then. What do you think of the starfaring life now?"

"Hectic. And *adhe* help me, confusing."

"Sometimes. Inclined to change your mind?"

"I cannot. Will you return to your clan?"

"I cannot. I'm sorry."

"As am I. I think I will know what not to do, though, when I get there," said Cian Canbhei. "I've had a good teacher. Perhaps it is possible to serve the Consortium and yet remain true to my blood."

"Perhaps it is. Creac knows, I may not have made the wisest choices I could make if a mewling infant like yourself could point out my mistakes to me. I could wish I had found such a wise middle ground."

"Perhaps you yet can."

"No. I won't go out there again."

"Not there." Cian pulled the blunted knife and its scabbard from his belt. "I will not need this where I'm going," he said. "But it might have some sentimental value for my sisters. Take it to them."

Óin looked at the knife but raised no hand to take it. "Just like that?"

"And tell them how you came by it."

"I couldn't—"

"They are not Ceiragh, but it is an honorable clan."

148

"No. . . ."

"They are not Ceiragh. You don't have to be *that* brave to tell the truth to strangers."

"That's true, isn't it?" He reached up, and Cian released the knife to his grip.

The younger *gal-adheni* stood. "The Canbhei have lost a Canbhei who was not quite a coward," he said. "It may be that they will welcome a Ceiragh who is not quite a hero." He turned and walked out through the unsheltered door, and the storm swallowed him instantly.

It is a thin trail that climbs a rocky hillside. In good weather, passersby sometimes look up and see the weathered stone hut it serves. Few bother to make the awkward climb, and of the few who do, all say that no one lives there now.

HOSPITAL STATION

James White

A vast hospital complex floating in space, built to
cater for the medical emergencies of the galaxy.
There are patients with eight legs – and none;
stricken aliens that breathe methane or feed on
radiation; an abandoned baby that weighs half a ton.
And there are doctors and nurses to match, with a
bewildering array of tentacles, and mental powers
stretching all the way to telepathy.

Faced by the illnesses and accidents of the universe,
fired by the challenge of galactic medicine, O'Mara,
the hospital chief, and his crack team, including the
altogether human Conway, with his insatiable
curiosity, and Prilicla, the brilliant and fragile insect
telepath, battle to preserve life in all its myriad forms.

HOSPITAL STATION – the astonishingly inventive
saga of a vast hi-tech community, a cross between
an emergency clinic and a zoo.

FUTURA PUBLICATIONS
AN ORBIT BOOK
SCIENCE FICTION

ISBN 0–7088–8181–5

THE WILD SHORE

Kim Stanley Robinson

'Simply one of our best writers'
Gene Wolfe

'A powerful new talent'
Damon Knight

2047: for 60 years America has been quarantined after a devastating nuclear attack. For the small community of San Onofre on the West Coast, life is a matter of survival: living simply on what the sea and land can provide, preserving what knowledge and skills they can in a society without mass communications. Until the men from San Diego arrive, riding the rails on flatbed trucks and bringing news of the new American Resistance. And Hank Fletcher and his friends are drawn into an adventure that marks the end of childhood . . .

A stunning debut by a powerful new talent.

'There's a fresh wind blowing in THE WILD SHORE . . . welcome, Kim Stanley Robinson'
Ursula K. Le Guin

'Beautifully written . . . with a vivid depth rarely encountered in science fiction'
Washington Post Book World

FUTURA PUBLICATIONS
SCIENCE FICTION

ISBN 0–7088–8147–5

WORLDS APART

Joe Haldeman

For the inhabitants of the Worlds – the artificial
colonies orbiting silently through space – Earth was
finished. Devastated by nuclear war and now
ravaged by the after effects of horrific biological
weapons, the mother planet was torn apart.
Humanity's home would soon be gone forever.

But Earth would not loose its ties so easily. And for
Marianne O'Hara there was work to be done in the
ghastly ruins of the stricken planet before she could
at last, look outwards to the stars.

WORLDS APART, the second volume of the brilliant
trilogy of mankind's future by the award-winning
author of THE FOREVER WAR.

FUTURA PUBLICATIONS/AN ORBIT BOOK
SCIENCE FICTION

ISBN 0–7088–8121–1

A NOOSE OF LIGHT

A magical new fantasy of the Arabian nights

Seamus Cullen

On a bare desert hillside overlooking a glittering city, an old man sits, keeping silent vigil. No man knows how long he has sat there, nor how old Anwar is . . .

But his tranquil life is soon to end, for there are those who would use him for their own ends: offering him to the people as the new prophet. And the Djmin Hawwaz wants Anwar's soul, while his brother Hutti plays dangerous games with mortal girls. When the beautiful Maryam comes to Anwar for advice in avoiding an unwelcome marriage, he sends her to Mecca. Baffled, she obeys his instruction to become a prostitute – and sets in motion a bizarre sequence of events, turning the worlds of human and demon alike upside-down.

A NOOSE OF LIGHT

Sensual, exotic, humorous and magical: an enchanting fantasy of an enchanted land.

FUTURA PUBLICATIONS
FANTASY/AN ORBIT BOOK

ISBN 0–7088–8178–5

interzone

SCIENCE FICTION AND FANTASY

Quarterly   £1.50

● *Interzone* is the only British magazine specializing in SF and new fantastic writing. We have published:

BRIAN ALDISS	M. JOHN HARRISON
J.G. BALLARD	GARRY KILWORTH
BARRINGTON BAYLEY	MICHAEL MOORCOCK
MICHAEL BISHOP	KEITH ROBERTS
ANGELA CARTER	GEOFF RYMAN
RICHARD COWPER	JOSEPHINE SAXTON
JOHN CROWLEY	JOHN SLADEK
PHILIP K. DICK	BRUCE STERLING
THOMAS M. DISCH	IAN WATSON
MARY GENTLE	CHERRY WILDER
WILLIAM GIBSON	GENE WOLFE

● *Interzone* has also published many excellent new writers; graphics by **JIM BURNS, ROGER DEAN, IAN MILLER** and others; book reviews, news, etc.

● *Interzone* is available from specialist SF shops, or by subscription. For four issues, send £6 (outside UK, £7) to: **124 Osborne Road, Brighton BN1 6LU, UK.** Single copies: £1.75 inc p&p.

● American subscribers may send $10 ($13 if you want delivery by air mail) to our British address, above. All cheques should be made payable to *Interzone*.

● "No other magazine in Britain is publishing science fiction at all, let alone fiction of this quality." *Times Literary Supplement*

- -

To: **interzone** 124 Osborne Road, Brighton, BN1 6LU, UK.

Please send me four issues of *Interzone*, beginning with the current issue. I enclose a cheque/p.o. for £6 (outside UK, £7; US subscribers, $10 or $13 air), made payable to *Interzone*.

Name _____

Address _____

_____